Sam Smith

# Sister Blister

Online Originals

**Sister Blister**
First published in 1999
by Online Originals
London and Bordeaux

Copyright © Sam Smith 1999

ISBN 1-84045-047-9

How heal the body of the phantom ill,
which started in the womb?

**Tesshu**
(14th century Japanese poet)

# 1

Dear Sister Clare,

They suggested that I write to you. What, though, to say to someone dead? What to say to someone who's never been truly alive?

I know, if I keep trying, I'll warm to it. Right now, though, I can't think of a thing to write. Or I can—I can think of lots—but not a starting point.

Ironical this, in light of my recent profession, that I should be in need of this kind of help. My kind of help. Being a provider of that kind of help I am, of course, beyond that kind of help, beyond my kind of help. Which is why I'm writing to you—you don't exist—I can therefore neither read nor feed your reactions.

So here I am, this time, dear sister Clare ...

How to start?

Where to start?

All my life, sister, all that I've been, all that I've known, has been crowding up to the edge of the future. And that future has always been an abyss, a chasm; and I've been looking for a way to get across to a side I can't see, can only imagine ... Looking across at what will be, at what I will be ...

Now, suddenly (if suddenly's the word—this crept up on me like night), these past few weeks I've turned my back on the future, on that becoming, and I've been looking out over the huge anchor of my past, have been made to feel the sheer iron dragging force of it ...

And you are part of my past, sister Clare, a substantial part of it. My present too.

I've got my starting point.

I'm an Acceptor now. It came about after the accident.

I was down the hospital all the time. Just waiting. Baby Bonny was killed outright, but Darren lived on for four days more. Never recovered consciousness. Neither did Fay. Although her coma lasted months. (They were talking of replacing so many of her organs that, come the end, just bothering with one didn't seem worth it.)

In the meantime I was down the hospital lots. Safest place for me to be. Police were in attendance—waiting for their two witnesses to recover. At least to start with. Nobody was going to have a second bite at me in there. And by the time the police were withdrawn I'd taken care of it anyway. Which left me just sat around the hospital day after day.

Marilyn and Ollie, of course, blamed me for the bomb. Angry at me, crying over their mother, they couldn't stay in the same room for long. (Marilyn and Ollie are grown up now. Were grown up then—it's only two years ago.)

Bonny and Darren were the babies, which is why it hit the headlines. 'Mob Bomb Kills Babies'. Their being babies was why they were with Fay when I dropped them off at the garage to pick up the car. Fay was going to take Darren on to playschool. He climbed into the back. Fay did up his seatbelt, then strapped Bonny into the safety seat in the front. Darren being in the back he didn't catch so much of the blast. Which is why he lived that much longer. The bomb was on the gearbox casing—between Bonny and Fay. Fay, leaning away—over the ignition to start it—seatbelt not done up, door not yet closed—she probably wanted to listen to the engine as that's why it'd been in the garage—she was blown out of the car. She lost her lower left leg right there: rest of the injuries were internal. Baby Bonny got slammed around inside, wouldn't have known what hit her. Nor did I know. I drove on into town thinking what I had to do next, found the police waiting for me when I got home.

This pretending is hard to sustain. This double pretending. Pretending to write to you, pretending you don't already know, when you, being inside me, already know all these things. (I can write this here: no-one but you and I will ever read it, will ever be able to read it. So I can tell you now, what you already know, that you are inside me. And there is a sense of release in saying this, the unstated. As if aloud.)

You have always been inside me sister. I have carried you from our birth. Every step of the way you've been with me. But, for the sake of this exercise, let us go back to assuming that you don't know. Might not know. Might not. You've been gone my forever. When, precisely, did your awareness end?

No. Let's not go too deep into this. Else I might talk myself out of writing to you altogether. And I miss you Clare. I've always missed you. (Stated, here, that's a new realisation.)

On with the story. As if a story ...

Consequence of the bombing was that I was alone in the hospital. I sat and I waited. I read the newspapers. I read magazines. Month after month. I was a hospital fixture.

You know what hospitals are like—all square lines, white lights, plastic seats, half-drunk cups of coffee ... I used to sit in the room with Fay and her breathing machines, or outside, smile back at the nurses, drink my coffee, sit beside other relatives new to their tragedy, listen to their stories ... And those relatives had to tell their stories ...

When, finally, they switched Fay off—not on the day exactly, but roundabout then—one of the nurses, who'd recently been on a grief-counselling course, suggested that I should do it too. She'd been watching me with the other relatives. "To help yourself help others," she said. I looked for ulterior meanings of course, said that I'd think about it, took her card.

Back in the house, nowhere to go every day, it was lonely. And all so pointless. Mal and Ollie only phoned to abuse me, cry at me—I certainly couldn't persuade them to 'accept'. Not even after I'd been on the course; and the tutor had decided that I wasn't exactly suited to grief counselling—probably because I've caused so much of it—but that I would make an excellent Acceptor. Which I am.

Get this straight—I don't cure people. I don't set out to 'cure' people. (Nowadays the belief that every problem has a solution leads to more problems than any other.) No, I simply try to lead people to an acceptance.

My job (part-time) is to sit in a room with two not-very-soft sofas and help the traumatised to come to terms with their pasts. With pasts that aren't often that remarkable. Just personal.

Each of us, sister, each of us thinks our lives exceptional. By common consent mine is. It isn't the only one though. There have been other lives like mine. Then there are the outwardly ordinary lives people can lead while beset with the most horrendous histories and guilts, obsessions and bizarre fears ... I listen, I wonder, and I accept.

Although a lot of it is beyond me, I'm good at what I do in that room with two sofas. Probably because no-one thinks me 'good' in any other sense, consequently there's no shame in confessing to me. So they confess anything and everything.

Confession is an odd thing. (I'm discovering as I write this.) Many people will readily give the appearance of confession—admitting to crimes, to sins—but will admit to no shame that might be thought, by themselves, to be unconventional. By public reputation, however, I'm a bastard. The frightened, the fantasists, have projected onto me acts of gothic extravagance. Nothing therefore, so the reasoning goes, can possibly surprise me. So to me they can confess everything. Although a few say, "You'll think a little thing like this silly ..." I reassure them not: size is always perception. What I usually open with is, "What happened to you?" And that's often all that I have to say. And I sit there on my sofa and let them talk.

The relief of some of them, just finding someone in this compartmentalised world they can talk to about anything. Some days it's like being sprayed with a hosepipe, a flow of words you could duck under.

Although some talkers can get stuck on one detail, one aspect, it's not often tedious. Even in just these couple of years I've had some interesting cases, a variety of traumas— warfare, family abuse, persecution, torture, freakish accidents... Wrong place wrong time is the hardest of all to reconcile. Or, having been the only one to walk away from the wreckage, they have got themselves caught up in the continual self-examination and re-examination of survivors, a constant questioning of the past—why them?

Why me?

You, sister, are my trauma.

You, sister, are my Acceptor. I'm going to tell you what happened to me.

# 2

Dear Sister Clare,

This is hopeless. I'll have to tell you everything. It's the only way. We'll have to pretend that you don't already know.

Here is where I spend most of my time. So I'll tell you about here.

This is my place. My made paradise. The bell-jar of my being.

From where I'm sitting now I can see the lake. It picks up colours from the sky. Changes throughout the day. Produces some odd effects. One showery day the whole arch of a rainbow was upside-down in the lake, but couldn't be seen in the sky from here.

Overcast now, the lake has the thin blue-white of skimmed milk.

The windows in this room overlooking the lake are from floor to ceiling. I won't bother telling you about the house though. Except, to get the best views, we had the living room and kitchen put upstairs, the bedrooms downstairs. For the rest ... Although Fay and I designed it, although this building bears the molecular imprint of our thoughts, it is not a changing thing, not—like the garden—a living thing.

Like other houses I've lived in one learns to live with a house, any house, the way it has become—the crooked curtain, the squeaking door, the whistle and song of the water in the pipes.

Little of that in this house. Here is perfect. And perfection has no character. It is kept perfect by the meticulous habits of a single man, is kept sterile by the domestic clearing-away rituals of a lonely man. (Have no pity sister—loneliness is most often deserved.)

The lake is the flat heart and soul of this property, its liquid crystalline centre. The house we had built at its upper end. Ideally we'd have liked to have had the house looking down the length of the lake, but that would have meant the foundations straddling the feeder stream, which would have meant us being too close to water and summer's mosquitos, in which case we might just as well have built at the lake's edge.

We didn't. Now, on the slope between us and the top end of the lake, is mostly grass and ground-cover. It used to be lawn; these days though I can't be bothered to cut it. I got some greylag geese once to keep the garden down, with the idea that they'd double as alarms. But they made a noise all the time—got on my nerves—and I could never tell whether they were raising the alarm or not. And their greasy green goose shit got trodden upstairs and down.

So now, up this top end by the house, I'm cultivating low ground-cover, mostly a deep purple; and down by the lake I'm leaving a long strip of grass for the wild black geese that winter over. They honk, don't hiss and gaggle. (I am not going to import animals here again. Whatever comes over the wall now will come of its own choice.)

All the rest of the way round the lake is woodland. Willows and alders by the lake rise up to a stand of silver birch, then a dark glinting mass of holly, then a clump of rook-infested cedars. I've also got a couple of big oaks here and there, and a few big beeches, some plane trees.

Radiating out from the house are line-of-sight avenues cut through the woodland. In every direction I can look almost down to the wall. The wall encircles the whole garden. Outside the wall is woodland too.

Along the outer edge of the wall, angled out, I've got a roll of razor wire. Along the top inside of the wall is an electrified strand. The two alloy gates are electronically controlled, have an independent electrical supply. They are doubled up within their own fence, like in a safari park, so that no-one can slip through with any incoming car, dodge off into the undergrowth. If they managed to get through the first gate they'd have to wait—exposed—with the car. It could be done; but it'd require some nerve.

Between the gates and the house is a low wooded hill. The garden is not overlooked. I have privacy here.

The lake stream is piped under the wall—in and out of the garden. No casual visitors, other than animals, come here unless I want them here. Although I know that I am unable to stop a determined intruder.

I guard here, sister, because here is beautiful, is my made paradise.

I guard this garden, sister, because I am inside it. And there are people who want me destroyed. (Not any one individual in particular who wants me destroyed, just somebody who will one day see me as an impediment. Personality doesn't enter into my probable demise.)

Each season here, sister, has its delights. Spring especially. In spring, from the house down to the lake, the slope is golden with daffodils. Ripples flowing orange into ripples at sunset.

Or, the rain pock-marking the lake, the daffodils stand, like wet sailors in yellow oilskins, all with their backs to the wind.

Or, from around the other side of the lake, the black glass of the house and the white mirror of the lake seem pressed apart by a fist of yellow.

Within the woodland, apart from the radial sight-lines, are three circular paths. (My only gardening these days—with buzz-saw, strimmer and secateurs—is to keep all of these paths open.) One path winds around the lakeside trees. The next is half-way up to the wall. The third path is just inside the wall.

Along all these paths I've cleared glades. Some I've planted with yellow, some with mauve and white crocuses. Always a pleasure, every spring, to re-discover them. A glade of sorrel too, one of blue wood anemones. One glade I planted with corns of candy-pink cyclamin for early autumn. Summers I have two glades of reedy yellow and orange montbretia.

Primroses, cowslips, bluebells; always the wood has something new to offer. In summer it is speckled with birdsong. Squirrels come of their own accord. Or were already here. Sit flicking their tails at me.

I've made garden seats here and there, knocked them together out of prunings. I was sat reading on one of those seats last summer and a squirrel stopped on the seat right beside me. I showed it to you. It made a note of our stillness, then went on.

Remember that quietness?

I had a man worked for me once. Not here. He had a record as a hard man. I had him marked down as quietly mad. Was always sober, never shouted his mouth off. He made no secret that he had an allotment. I paid him plenty, but he kept on his allotment. Nor could you take the mick out of him—wouldn't rise to it. One day I was really pissed off. Just pissed off—with everything and nothing. He said to me, "If you want to be happy for a day—get drunk. If you want to be happy for a year—get married. If you want to be happy for life—get a garden."

He was right. Here, always, every season, there's a delight. A swarm of black and white butterflies rising out of a sun-filled glade. Even orange fungus can startle me into taking notice. Or bright red holly berries, rosehips shouting to be eaten. This is the life you could, you should have had. I have tasted, smelled it for you. Now I'm writing it for you.

Down at the bottom end of the lake there are yellow flags, moorhens and their chicks, the croak of fat frogs, dragonflies like bossy helicopters. And the smell of wet.

The lake is now my only other labour in this garden. Beginning of every winter I take out the punt and grapple, drag the year's new weed out. If I didn't the sides would silt up, grow over in no time, and the lake would become just a tiny stream filtering through a tangled marsh. And the lake is central to this place. I worry about the lake when I'm gone.

When I'm gone. When I'm gone, sister, what will happen to all the slowly acquired knowledge of this gardener? To this trial and error of years? Too much by far to tell you. And who would you tell, sister?

You could have come here with me and been safe. You could have danced here as light as the swallows that dip to the lake—each rising spread-tailed from its made circle. Oh life then is almost wonderful.

It is wonderful here. I used to organise treasure hunts for Marilyn and Ollie. They'd disappear for hours, make camps. Freedom for them when we came here. Baby Bonny and Darren never got a chance of course.

Autumn when they died. The sumac across the lake red like a slap, poplars silver and black. Gales ricochet down the pathways, make eddies, which leave tossed heaps of silver, black and gold. The breath steaming out of our mouths is when we can see we're alive. I've told you this before, on our walks, through my garden. "See. We're alive." You hanging there for a moment, seen through, shapeless.

I've just got back from a walk. I went looking for things to tell you. Or was it that, telling you of them, made me want to go and see them all again?

Anyway I found an old seat and shelter I'd made—rustic, to not look out of place—all smashed up. Not as an accident, but out of malice.

Whoever was responsible has been climbing up a big tree outside and coming across on one of its boughs, then transferring to one of my trees. And they've been doing it for some time—on both trees are old and new marks. And they've deliberately snapped some birch saplings too, have left beer cans lying around. This has to stop. A gun and spade are called for.

# 3

Guest gone,
I stroke the brazier,
talk to myself.

**Shozan** (1717-1800)

I know you're there sister Clare.

I know you're there now; and I know you know all about me. You've been there for every act, for every move, watching.

Always watching. Always listening. You know my thoughts. At times you are my thoughts sister.

You are there; believe me Sister Clare. You are there, the original acceptor. You judge nothing. Just see. Just hear. Just know. How much, though, do you know about yourself? At first-hand? Not through me. How much?

You know my thoughts. Are they, though, coherent enough to tell you?

We are one, you and I. You know, therefore, that I sometimes have to explain myself to myself. I'll assume—for the purpose of here—that you too live on that level of understanding. I will tell you, sister, about you.

I am the only other human being you have touched. (I won't count our mother: she was just the noises outside our womb sac—engine drum of her heart, sea-sounds of her digestion and circulation.) You, sister Clare, touched me in the womb. You curled your little fingers around my wrist. (This is not morbid fancy on my part. Our mother had a convex triangular photo, ultra-sound scan, blown up poster-size on her bedroom wall. In the cardboard album of other shots, not so clear, we seem to be embracing.)

You died in there sister Clare. Two or three days before term. (They estimated the two or three days from my birth those two or three days later.) Only I, inside that placenta, knew that you'd gone sister. Only I knew that in your going your spirit passed into me.

How could it have been otherwise? Touching, rotating weightlessly about one another, knees and elbows nudging, heads bumping, we built up in that breathed amniotic fluid our one morphic field. Those thought-lines bound us in there and, regardless of death, bind us still.

Every child born is a new world sister. From day one I had to be both our worlds.

When I was about twelve I came of the belief that I had to live twice as hard, do twice as much, for the both of us. Back then I kissed boys for you. Had to beat some of them to make sure they didn't tell. They didn't tell.

I've lived my whole life half for you sister—imagining you there, the mirror opposite, seeing out through your eyes at your mirror opposite, myself, cock tucked between my legs.

At our every birthday you've been there—in pink party frocks to begin with, jeans and a pout later. (Our mother crying, especially if a crowd.) Now, like me, you'd be tall, good bones, thick hair. How identical were we sister Clare?

Not very. Not once we were beyond the womb. My extinct, my non-existent sister. My anima, my alter-ego, my dead and not-gone sister.

I've lived my whole half-life for you sister. From the moment of our birth. Imagine our mother screaming, and enjoying her screams. (I've watched her give birth in films— all waxy sweat and hoarse imprecations.) Imagine me pink and plump with life, you grey and blue and small with death. Both of us slapped down there in a pool of crimson blood between her slack white thighs.

Me they put in a perspex crib with a blue blanket. Your tiny body was taken away and put into a small polished coffin. You had to be given a name for the paperwork. Clare your corpse became. Clare your memory became. Imagine all the weeping and the wailing at the service. Made no difference: you were already inside me.

You were outside too, an absence. Something for new people ever after to be told off, in a whisper, "He's one of twins. She died."

So you became then, not my companion inside, not my self-watcher, but an external weight, a deadweight, that I had to carry around. You, sister, became like a long blister down my spine—the skin numb and dead on the outside, the malforming weight of the lymphatic fluid inside. Liquefied you. Always there, sister blister, wobbling about on my back, to be knocked against, to get in the way when dressing for a new day. Always there.

Sister blister sister blister sister blister. It only needs one open sore upon a body for the whole of it to feel unclean. Sister blister.

I hated you for dying. You made me different. (Before I didn't want not to be like everyone else.) All my childhood, sister blister, you sat on my head like an iron frog. No-one wanted to be friends with me because I was whispered to be not normal, to be not complete.

I was more than me. I had the ghost of you, sister

blister, walking like a mist inside my shadow.

Oh sister I'm sorry I said that. Not your fault. I know now—from watching Mal and Ollie grow—that I was too keen, too eager. My greed for friends, my raw need for them, frightened them away. I had to absorb them, replace you. And when they couldn't satisfy that need, when they didn't become you, I despised them, found reasons to despise them.

I did pop the blister of you occasionally sister. Let you drain away into forgetfulness. Usually when we'd moved. But, like with every new pair of shoes you buy, with every new way of life I tried, with every new kind of person I tried to be, up came the blister again. Come the end, sister blister, you were the only thing that moved on with me.

And you, sister blister, you watched that every move. Did you pity me? I felt that you alone were sorry for me. I was sorry for you. I didn't want you to have died.

I doubly watched the everyday for you—rainbows and sunsets. And I stole knickers and dressed up in our mother's clothes—for you. I kissed boys for you.

You were there at every kill.

Ours has been a strange life sister blister.

I miss you still.

# 4

Hillcrest woodland falls to fields, a farm, and onto a small
village of old houses built around a stream and a bridge.
Woodland surrounds the village. More fields, level now,
lead to a railway line hemmed with brambles. Next to it is
the circling grey of a motorway junction; and next to the
junction the flat shed roofs of an industrial estate. Which
leads into a housing estate of squared streets and small box
houses, each with its red tile roof. This was once called a
council estate, now is defined as 'Social Housing'. Mostly,
though, it is referred to by the name of the area—
Hambrook.

Successive town authority's have tried to rid
Hambrook of its local reputation. Lately they have installed
'traffic-calming' slaloms and speed ramps. (The boy racers
have changed to scramble bikes.) Before that the council
funded, block by block, extensive renovation—older houses
even being knocked down and rebuilt in modern styles,
along with a package of modern socio/psychological know-
how—different pattern paving and bricks delineating the
territory and responsibility of each house, each yard.

Poverty though creates its own stigmas; and where
elsewhere anti-social behaviour and poor services would not
be tolerated, here the people—de-valued—do not have
sufficient self-respect to dare complain. So cars continue to
get dismantled on the pavements, music blares into the
night, the buses run late, dogs crap where they will, and the

inhabitants' children practise burglary on each other.

Newcomers, seeing the state of the place, and being poor believing they don't matter, they accept this as the status quo and adapt their behaviour accordingly. (Or, unable to suffer the unsociable behaviours of their neighbours any longer, their complaints ignored by the understaffed police and the underfunded council, their frustration erupts into violent confrontation. Which leads to retaliation, which adds to the reputation of the neighbourhood.)

Fat Steve Flinthorn lives on the corner of one of the outermost boxes, almost not part of the estate. He parks his work van almost in the drive, the back end level with the two brick gate posts. The gates being open he watches over it from his lounge and bedroom windows. (Though most teenage trouble on the estate is down near the iron-grilled shops, where the skateboarders use the speed-bumps as take-off ramps and the girls hang around outside the two phone boxes and the video shop with its three arcade games.)

Steve Flinthorn's son, Dan, no longer hangs around outside the shops. Steve doesn't know where Dan hangs out now. Steve doesn't know  where Dan is now. Mary, Dan's mother, is worried. She has made Steve go out this evening and look for him.

Short and tubby, unused to walking these streets this time of day, Steve feels unable to approach the quick boys on their hard rattling skateboards. Most, anyway, are younger than Dan: Steve doubts that Dan would even speak to them. And, lest they foulmouthed accuse him of impropriety, Steve doesn't dare approach the skinny girls sucking on their cigarettes.

Steve buys a packet of liquorice allsorts in the video

shop. He goes the long way home, walks slowly eating the sweets.

Mary Flinthorn is a cleaner in an old people's home. Most evenings, the dinner cooked, washing-up done, she sits curled on the sofa, works through her usual week of soaps and quiz shows. This evening she walks around with a yellow cloth nervously wiping at already clean windowsills.

"For chrissake siddown!" her daughter Julie snaps at her. "Little sod'll be home before you know it."

Julie is eighteen, hair permed and bleached, voice flattened, is doing keyboard skills and business studies at Tech. She is three years older than Dan. Like him she despises their dithering parents.

Mary flinches from Julie's hard voice. Leaving the living room, Julie crouched in the armchair, Mary goes up to the front bedroom. On the way, noticing herself doing it, she wipes the yellow cloth over the varnished bannister.

From the bedroom window Mary sees Steve squeezing in the gateway past the white van. She goes fumbling and bumping quickly back down the stairs.

"For fuck's sake." Julie says at the noise.

Mary ducks her head, grabs the front of Steve's thin jacket,

"Where is he?"

Steve, pulling against her grabbing of his jacket, seems to give a shrug.

"No-one seen him?" Mary's ginger-blue eyes try to read his face.

"No-one."

"No-one?"

Pulling from her he shrugs again. Mary releases his jacket and, taking a deep breath, makes herself upright,

"That's it then." Holding the yellow cloth like a gauntlet she takes it into the kitchen and throws it into the stainless steel sink. "I'm going to the police." She opens the stair cupboard for her coat.

"Now hang on." Steve blocks the kitchen doorway.

"Don't be so bloody daft Mother!" Julie shouts.

"I know something's happened. I know." Mary pushes her arms into her coat.

"You don't know. You can't know." Steve shakes his head, "Look he ..."

"I'm going!" Mary shouts at him, chin puckering, tears reddening her eyes.

Steve doesn't know what to say to stop her, can only repeat what he's said before,

"What if it's something to do with the police? What if we drop him in it?"

"Then it's his own stupid fault. He should've let us know. And at least they'll tell me. Won't they? They'll tell me." Coat on Mary stares at Steve standing in the kitchen doorway, doesn't seem to know how to get past him.

Dan, at fifteen, has already made several court appearances, appears to hold it in contempt. Looking older than fifteen, bigger already than Steve, he's been caught selling solvents and cigarettes to younger children, been done twice for stealing and selling bikes, has even been in a crashed, stolen car. Steve is frightened of what his son may do next. He wasn't like Dan at his age, doesn't know what made Dan like it. He does know that Dan doesn't want him or his mother going to the police.

"You certain that bike he's got is his?" he asks Mary.

"Says he traded it off some kid in school. Give a dog a bad name ..."

"Dad!" Julie shouts from her living room chair. "Dad!"

louder.

"What?" Steve doesn't want to leave the doorway.

"Go round and see his friend, wossisname. He'll know where the little sod is."

"Who's that?" Steve asks over his shoulder.

"You know. Thingy."

"Who?" Steve asks Mary.

"She means Martin Thurlow's boy."

"They still friends?"

"Always sneaking off together." Julie shouts. "Coupla poofs."

If Dan was here now he'd be shouting an insult back at her—about disgusting things she did with boys—and Julie would go running up the stairs screaming swear words at him, telling her mother and father to go wash his dirty fucking mouth out. Mary would turn up the television. Steve would go into the back garden. Or out into the garage to work on the mustard yellow mini he is slowly restoring. (When it is finished, children left home, he and Mary are going to drive to Scotland in it.)

Dan isn't here to shout at Julie.

"You go round and see Martin Thurlow." Mary starts to take off her coat, "If his boy don't know where our Dan is, then I'll go to the police. Go on."

# 5

Martin Thurlow is a big man with big hands. From infancy, having always been bigger than those his own age, Martin Thurlow has got his own way, has thus got into the habit of domination.

Martin Thurlow dominates his small factory floor. Not that he is in charge, nor that he is shop-steward rebellious: Martin Thurlow's one philosophy is that no-one is going to tell him what to do. To this end he has made himself good at his job. No-one is going to tell him how to do it. He tells others what to do. Boss and union know that if they have his sanction their lives will be easier.

Big Martin Thurlow will not try to become a boss, because—were he to get promoted, were he to become a part of any management structure—then Martin would be subject always to the approval of the manager a step above him; and thus Martin would be made aware, always, of being dominated.

Likewise, if Martin were to play an active part in union affairs, he would be subject to union rules, those rules decided upon by the very people he ordinarily dominates. Martin, therefore, seeks neither.

Although he is presently little more than a machinist on a short assembly line, Martin continues to call himself a craftsman. He sees himself as a man of independent mind; and he is contemptuous both of the work that he does and of his fellow workers, and of the wages they are all paid for that work.

Before this factory Martin worked for a garden furniture firm, which work he also despised—deliberately clumsy, he called it. Nor was the pine kitchen furniture job much better—production line assembly, each turning out his own part. And before that the best he could get was architraving on building sites; or, worse, shuttering for concrete. And always working for different people, with different people ... He'd hated that.

To support his self-esteem Martin has converted his garage into a workshop. (Martin doesn't own a car, can't drive—wouldn't be told.) The garage is where Martin does what he calls his 'real' work.

Like all carpenters Martin aspires to be a cabinet maker. His house—same size same estate as Steve Flinthorn's—is furnished with products from his garage workshop. A slatted three-piece suite in the living room, a lathe-turned light switch pull in the bathroom, a leaf-carved newel post ... Martin's furniture dominates the house.

Martin is scathing of his neighbour's taste in furniture, the prices they pay for machine-made tat just because it's in the catalogues. (Hambrook neighbours may acquire work from Martin's garage workshop only on commission. Martin will not risk the rejection of unsold pieces, submit himself to the power, to the domination, of the purchaser.)

Steve Flinthorn knows Martin Thurlow—discounting the last time the two boys were in trouble; and then he and Martin didn't mention it—only as the big loud man seen occasionally on the benches at work, as the big brash man who has a few rare times helped him load the van. Grumpy Martin was then impervious to Steve's cheeriness.

"He's a miserable git." Steve had said to one of the others the first time— after Martin had gone.

"Should try working with him," the other man had said.

Martin doesn't go to the pub, even for darts matches, which is when Steve goes, has his own arrows. (Martin couldn't dominate a pub, would always feel his domination challenged by the next stranger coming through the pub door—and even a local pub landlord tries to bring in new custom. Alcohol also removes Martin's dominion of himself. Martin prides himself on being teetotal, on being in control.)

Approaching Martin Thurlow's house Steve Flinthorn is nervous. A fawn car goes past, stereo a tight drum in the door, bumping out the beat of Steve's heart.

Home-made tubs of white and red flowers stand on the ribbed concrete of the unused driveway. The small front garden beside it has brick paths in a French cross between the four triangular rose beds. (Martin sprays the rose bushes for black spot before coming to work mornings.) A passion flower has been trained up a carved trellis.

Having pressed the doorbell, waiting at the front door, Steve notices an ivy stem and leaves carved into the trellis. He is leaning forward for a closer look when the door is opened by Tina Thurlow, Martin's wife.

Tina still has on her supermarket green-white striped uniform.

"You haven't seen Dan?" Steve says, remembering to apologise. "Sorry to trouble you, but ... well, Dan hasn't been home a couple of days. His mum's worried. Simon in?"

"No." Tina has been blank-faced watching him, now steps back. "Come in. I'll call Martin."

Tina has a large chest balanced by a big backside.

"Martin!" she yells into the house. "Martin!"

Tina is loud in the supermarket, not usually around

Martin, who emerges frowning from the kitchen. In acknowledgement of Steve he unsmiling lifts his chin,

"What's up?"

Steve Flinthorn likes working for Sweets Suites. All his previous driving jobs have had the pressure of a regular round behind them. Sweets' addresses, although some are to the same warehouses, same suppliers, are mostly different. And he enjoys being out on his own in the van, singing to himself as he tootles along, with a smile answering the hand-signals and headlight courtesies of other drivers. Steve also likes being cheerful and obliging to the customers he meets on behalf of Sweets Suites.

Martin Thurlow is polite to no-one. Martin likes nothing better than to get one over on his boss, to argue the point with his workmates.

"Like a cup of tea?" Tina says to Steve as she turns to squeeze past Martin in the narrow hall. (It is part of their marital agreement that she has to remind 'the big lummox' of his social ps & qs.)

"Cup of tea?" Martin makes the question his, returns ahead of Steve to the kitchen.

Steve is left to shut the front door, follows them.

"It's Dan," Steve says to Martin by way of explanation. Martin is already sat back down on the far side of white wooden table. (Formica table top in Steve's own kitchen.) "Thought he might be here—with your Simon?"

"Simon?" Martin shakes his head. "No ..."

Tina is plugging in the kettle, getting a mug and a tea-bag down, her back to Steve.

"Thought he was round your place." Martin says. "Asked anywhere else?" he indicates a wheel-backed chair for the still-standing Steve.

Steve sits down without passing comment on the chair.

"Last we know," Steve's worry seems to bounce inside himself, "Dan was with Simon."

"In some scrape." Martin dismisses Steve's worry— unseemly in a man.

"Yea but that time—before—when they got in that trouble, police were round straightaway. Have to. They're minors."

The two sets of parents have not talked together of that 'trouble'.

"In that case they're alright." Martin says. "No police, no trouble."

"Mary wants me to go to the police. Report Dan missing."

Martin and Tina have glanced to one another.

"Danny Boy!" Martin gives a big laugh. "Our Danny Boy can take care of himself. Can't he?" He does not expect to be contradicted.

"We thought Simon'd stayed over with you." Tina says: Simon and Dan have never stayed overnight in each other's houses. "You know what the two of them are like ..."

Trying to look into Steve's face to see what he is thinking she places the mug of tea on the white wood of the table before him. (Martin has a raffia place mat under his plate, a raffia coaster under his mug. He looks at the mug's unglazed rim on the table's unprotected grain.) Tina asks Steve if he takes sugar. Steve does, but—not seeing any to hand—feeling hot, he says, 'no thanks'.

Of the same age, growing up in the same place, and given their different backgrounds, there has been an inevitability about Dan and Simon becoming friends.

Dan, reacting against what he perceives as the anxious timidity of his mother and father—he calls it shit-taking— has become loud and pushy.

Simon, used to being told what to do by his father, feels on familiar territory with Dan—with the added benefit, in following Dan, that it places him conspicuously above his Hambrook contemporaries. Gets him into trouble too, but the kind of trouble generally respected around Hambrook, and which he wouldn't have dared without Dan. (Most Hambrook children are expected to be caught at least once shoplifting, possibly also caught misappropriating bikes. Simon and Dan have written off four cars, but been caught only the once.)

Both smoke.

Martin knows this, knows too that Simon disobeys him in other ways—despite being shouted at, despite being hit. Simon doesn't argue back—hasn't the words or the technique—doesn't physically resist the cuffs, or struggle against being held by the throat—he hasn't the strength—he just sneaks out and gets into trouble again. Tina tells her workfriends that her eldest boy is 'out of control'.

While Martin and Tina privately complain about Simon being led astray by Daniel Flinthorn, Martin also identifies with and defends Dan, approves of his loud shoving aside of the world, his contempt for all its values. Martin hopes for Dan that he too will find some saving skill, one that he can be proud of, so that his whole life may not be negative.

For his own son, for Simon, Martin hopes that some of Danny Boy's 'push' will rub off, that—eventually—of his own accord, Simon too won't give a shit what anyone else might think. (Martin used to call Simon a cry-baby when he was younger.)

Martin stares across the table at Steve, envying him his son, hating the fat face wrinkled around its worry, a creep's worry—that says it doesn't want to upset anyone.

"So when, exactly, did you last see Dan?"

"Two, three days ago." Steve is looking hotter, a dapple of sweat along his receding hairline.

"He stays out late. Both do. Not often all night. Never three nights like this."

Martin decides Steve talks like a woman: Steve is always chatting to the fussy old cow who works in the office.

"I'll ask Nate." Tina goes to the bottom of the stairs and shouts, "Nate!" Martin screws up one side of his face. "Nate!" Tina's shout is louder.

"Chrissake he's got his music on." Martin's voice booms out. "Go up and get him. Bloody deafen us, woman."

Grumbling about being on her legs all day (she works behind the delicatessen counter, cuts cheese and wears a white hat) Tina goes grunting and groaning up the stairs.

"Could've found themselves a couple of girlfriends." Martin says, "Flat of their own? Parents away?"

"No..." Steve shakes his head, sees Martin's frown deepen at being disagreed with. "Yea they could've. But the girls'd have to be older."

"Not if their parents are away."

"Who'll that be?"

"Not likely to tell us are they?"

"I think Mary's right." Loyalty makes Steve say, "Something's happened to them."

Martin, inwardly conceding lack of evidence, gives that last assertion serious consideration. Steve is relieved that Martin has decided that Simon is with Dan: he didn't want to think what to do on his own.

"If they're in some sort of scrape," Steve says again, "hiding up or something, I don't want to be the one who drops them in it. Specially if the police got no idea."

"Careful—letting your imagination run away with

you."

Upstairs Tina has been shouting about the bloody headphones.

"Your father wants to see you. Now!"

"Alright alright."

A skimming patter-patter of bare feet brings Nathan down the stairs. He comes shaven-headed and brown brazen-eyed into the kitchen.

"Yea?"

"You seen Simon?"

Nathan looks at Steve,

"What's up?"

"When you last see him?" Martin's voice has an edge of anger.

"I dunno."

Martin thinks his youngest son surly and disrespectful. Nathan has decided that his father is a bully. He doesn't like him.

"You know where they went?" Martin's voice is louder.

Nathan shakes his head. A shake that says he wouldn't tell even if he knew.

"Any idea would help." Steve says. "Would give us a clue. You see ... Dan's mum wants me to go to the police, report Dan missing. And I don't want to go getting him and Simon into trouble."

His father never explains to Nathan, just says This is this, This is that, "Do it." And it is more often wrong than not.

Nathan doesn't care about his brother Simon either— their father is a bully and Simon lets himself be bullied. Nathan thinks Simon is a creep. But he rates Dan. Rates him so much he can't understand what Dan sees in a creep like Simon. Nathan fights Simon, has twice made him cry;

although Simon more often backs off, goes into his own room shouting threats, slams the door. (Nathan himself cries when fighting—so angry is he. Cries not to be able to win easier. Cries not to be able to win. Not after he's been beaten. Dan has watched him, has said nothing.)

"I know where they could be," Nathan says to Steve.

Simon got off his bike and threw stones at Nathan to stop him following them. Nathan pretended to turn back; but, bent low over his handlebars—so they wouldn't see him over the tops of the hedges—he followed them.

"Where?" Martin says.

"Out past Estley Wood. There's a wall. They climbed up over it. I think they got a place in there."

"What kind of place?"

"Camp. Or something."

"You think," Steve says, "they could've stayed there?"

Nathan shrugs, arrogant, the teacher-softness of Steve's questions beginning to irritate him.

When he followed Dan and Simon he found their bikes before he did them. Then he had trouble climbing the tree, scared himself by the height. But he thought he saw them walking off into the woods the other side of the wall, branch ends moving where they passed.

The yellow and black signs saying 'Electric' on the wire along the top of the wall made him even more nervous. He could see how Dan and Simon had climbed across branch to branch, but didn't trust his own strength. So, clinging at times to the trunk, he climbed and slid back down the tree and, out of spite, let down Simon's back tyre. Having done that he couldn't then wait for them to come back, in case they didn't have a pump and knew it was him. Cold in the woods, feeling very alone, he rode quickly downhill and along to home.

Nathan is frightened now that they may have been caught because of his letting down Simon's tyre, then remembers that they came home that night and he recalls his thinking that one of them must have had a pump in his bag. Neither of them mentioned the flat tyre while he was listening.

"You know who that fucking wall belongs to?" Martin says to Steve. "You know who?"

"Who?" Steve shrugs his not knowing.

"That gangster. The one who's wife and kids got blown up."

"Him?" Steve thinks he remembers it being on the news.

"So there's fuck-all point in us going to the police. He'll have them in his pocket for certain."

"You reckon?"

"Course he has. He's a gangster. Everybody knows he's a gangster. And he lives there. If everybody knows he's a gangster why isn't he put inside?"

"Evidence?"

"Evidence my arse. He's paid someone off. And where did our two silly sods decide to trespass? His place."

"They wouldn't disappear just because they trespassed. Something else must've happened to them."

"Yea? What if our two pratts were doing a bit of burglaring? Wouldn't put it past 'em. Would you? Then we go to the law and say our two were last seen climbing over a wall into a private garden. Terrific eh?"

Tina has come sighing back down the stairs. The two men watch her move around Nathan to sit the weight of herself at the table. She has been into Simon's room. It was untidy. She started to pick clothes off the floor, but her back went stiff. She didn't want to sit down in there—only the bed to sit on and it is so low it would have been hard to get up off again—so she had come back downstairs.

"So what you going to do?" she asks Martin. "If they are in there? The police might very well want to take a look inside that gangster's house."

"Don't be so fucking daft woman. You're not telling me that if they wanted to take a look in there they wouldn't have done? Before now? Even the newspapers call him a gangster, say he has 'undesirable connections'. He ever sued them for libel? Do the police ever go thundering into his place in the middle of the night—like they do round here? Oh no. Obvious they're in his pocket."

"So what you going to do?" Tina says, "Leave 'em there?"

"No." Martin stands. "We're going to go up and have a look. You got Sweets' van?" he asks Steve. "We'll take that. Nate you come with us and show us where they got over. You sure his bike's not in the shed?"

"Don't think so." Nate says, excited by this unexpected outing.

"Get your shoes on and go check." Martin tells him.

Standing with them, Steve is about to say that he's not sure about taking the van, but he doesn't want to be argued into taking it, to be told that it's his son they're going to look for.

# 6

Steve is conscious of the odd picture the three of them must make in these flat Hambrook streets—his own little legs going fast under his belly to keep up with the big glowering Martin, with—behind them—Martin's youngest son lolloping along, even more self-conscious, his shaved head lowered and glancing side to side.

Finally they squeeze in between the brick gatepost and the van. (Coming home late sometimes Julie curses out loud to have to do it, then laughs—laughs really loud—with her friends. Cackling on and on.)

"I'll get the keys." Steve says.

Mary opens the door to him.

"What's happening?" She sees Martin.

Steve presses her aside as he passes her.

"Hello Martin." Mary says. They went to school together, though not in the same year. Mary is older. "What's happening? Are they together?"

"Think they might've got stuck." He says in a loud voice, comes closer to say, "Know that gangster? Lives out past Estley? His family got blown up in that car?"

Mary frowns: that wasn't the response she was expecting. Remembering the newspaper story, she nods. It was on the local news too.

"What about him?"

"Our two silly sods climbed the wall into his garden. Nate," he nods to Nathan, who stretches a grin, "saw where.

We're going up to check if they're still there."

"What if they're not?"

Martin turns his lips down, looks along the road. Nathan has been watching him, looks where he is looking. Sees nothing. Steve edges past them.

"Got to clear off the front seat," he says.

"You sure we shouldn't call the police now?" Mary steps after Steve, rubs at her own arms.

"Let's have a look up there first." Steve glances back to Martin. "Like Martin says they probably got stuck the other side of the wall. Just need a help out."

Yes, Mary thinks, maybe that'll be best. Best not to get anyone else involved. But, watching Steve get into the van and fuss with papers and a jacket on the passenger seat, Mary worries that the two men and the boy might get carried away with the excitement of all this chasing around.

At the same time she is relieved that Steve is at last doing something, not just grunting back at her when she tells him that she's worried. Like Steve, she doesn't want to get Dan into yet more trouble. He's not a good boy Dan, but he wasn't always like this. Lively, that was all. But which got him into trouble with those who wanted him to be still, at school. And give a dog a bad name ...

All these years of doing one stupid cleaning job after another, just to get by. And nearly there—a year to go and Dan'll be off their hands. Can find his own place, own job. Leave her and Steve to their own little ways; be like her Mum and her man—always off on a week's holiday here, a week's holiday there.

These last few days Mary has already got used to Dan not being here, to the quiet of his not being here. And she feels guilty for noticing how relaxed it all is, tells herself that she'd rather have her son home and safe, trouble and all.

Going back indoors, after the van's left, Mary gets to thinking that she doesn't understand authority, why it can't see that her son's not bad. What do teachers know of his life? What do courts know? She has sat there with him and listened to them talk and not known what they were talking about. Yes, best let the men sort it out. If they can.

# 7

Sister,
     Now that I've started these letters I can't stop.
Confession has become my curse. No sooner have I decided
to give up writing for the day, walk away, than I'm thinking
what more I can say. Must say. Say it now.
     Let's go back, sister blister, to assuming that you don't
know. That you, visitor from another galaxy, don't know a
thing about our two parents. About our two celebrated
parents.
     Just thinking about them, just bringing the two of
them into my mind, makes me angry. Even now.
     Why?
     My very first thought about our mother, my first sit-
down-and-think thought, rather than as a reaction to her—
and this as a small child—was that it would have been easier
for her if I too had died pre-birth. She could then, grief
over, have swiftly moved on to a new public role. But my
being there—living and growing and needing—I was more
than a hindrance, more than a reminder. Motherhood was
over: I was a continuing, unnecessary and changing constant
consideration, a permanent puzzle to her.
     Both our parents were actors. Let's get that clear.
Public and private actors. And I, their only child, was
career-neglected. Not in the sense that I was left alone at
home like Cinders, while they went off in tux and sequins to
glittering premieres. That part I actually enjoyed—glory by

association, smiling at the smiles, waving to the waves, blinking at the camera flash, cheering our parents being cheered.

The public face was the gliding swan on the surface that I, like everyone else, was conditioned to admire—which sort of thing reflects well on a child, a secondhand excitement. It was all the work leading up to that moment, all the time spent other than with this child, that this child resented.

My neglect came from our shimmering parents' furiously paddling feet, from their being busy with things more important than me. Scripts to be read, phone calls to be made, people and places to be seen, parts to be chased, projects to be involved in—all the hustle and politics of a successful actor's life.

No point going on about our father. His one positive part in our creation was nine months prior to my birth. And of that nine month prior moment, sister, his sperm loosed and swimming, I know nothing. Nor can it be of consequence to any human being to know the circumstance of their creation. No-one ordinarily needs to know how they were conceived. It cannot matter—even to me, and I want to know everything. A few mundane grunts and that is it, a new life has been created. Or, in our case, two. The mode of conception, however, unless it unsettles the mother—a rape for instance—cannot have any significance to the life that emerges nine months later. Or, in your case, the death.

Once born—although I could hardly know then that you were missing—I was lonely without you.

My birth, your death, upstaged our father, made his role subordinate to his wife's. His commitment to the marriage, anyway, was only partial—away a lot he had affairs while he was away. Had it not been for your death, sister blister, would he have left altogether? Did he stay only because, publicly, it would have looked bad to have dumped a grieving, a very publicly grieving, wife? Which is what her role became.

As if acting didn't occupy enough of her time, leaving little time for me; as if that wasn't enough, you, sister blister, you took the rest of our mother's mind and time.

Hard to tell with any actor what their genuine feelings are. Even for themselves: they're so used to thinking themselves into emotions, into producing effects. At first, I think, she probably did truly grieve for you. And when the support group contacted her I think she was genuinely grateful for their sympathy and understanding. (To be understood, I know now as Acceptor, is often more important than sympathy. Sympathy without understanding, sister, is like novocaine injected into the wrong gum.)

So grateful was our mother to the support group that, when they asked for her help in fund-raising, she leapt at the chance. It became her cause.

I've just been looking at the old footage. At the loads of it. Yet again.

I'm always surprised to find myself on that old footage. A babe-in-arms, then a toddler. And my being there, not for the audiences to delight in my innocence, not there as evidence of compensation, but as a poignant testament to what might have been, half of a possibility.

She was, she is, a good actress, our mother. Even now she can still bring a tear to my eye. Pure technique of course.

One moment she was there on every channel, on every chat-show sofa—good legs, our mother—with me clinging to the sofa's edge, sitting with a bump, banging into microphones, shouting out to the laughter of the adult audience ... Then I got too big, got sly and shy, and it was over.

Our mother got a season treading Shakespearian boards, and I got our first nanny. I was learning to talk then, to ask questions, to wonder where you were, sister. Our parents were too busy to notice my grief.

A child is not a person-proper, is still being formed. How can a child, barely articulate amongst highly articulate people, how can that child—a child more receptor than actor—how can that child be experiencing grief? How can that child express grief?

One nanny, a simple grunting girl despised by our mother, called me her poor lonely little man. Her sympathy, her noticing, didn't count, and I screamed her away from me.

I'll tell you now, sister, that all grief is the one grief. So when Fay, Darren and Baby Bonny were killed I ended up grieving, not for them, but for you again.

Odd, isn't it, that, as a makeshift cure for the grieving of you, they trained me as an Acceptor? And now, as a cure for being an Acceptor, for being overwhelmed with a world of others' troubles, they have sent me back to you.

I miss you sister. I miss you still.

# 8

Something that Steve does every morning without thinking, this evening has him in a sweat. As if it wasn't enough Martin and Mary standing like dummies silently watching him, he also has Nathan bumping around on the front seat, trying to look in the wing mirrors and blocking his view. He wants to shout at Nathan,

"Sit the fuck down!" Doesn't. Not with his dad standing there. Wouldn't, without his dad standing there.

Once the van is out in the road, Martin comes striding around the front, solemn and stern like a sheriff in a Western. Opening the door he tells Nathan, "Budge up."

Nathan is squashed thin and wriggling against Steve's side. The door is needlessly slammed. Mary, not wanting to be left stood on her own outside, is already scuttling back indoors.

"Tell us where to go," Martin tells Nathan.

"Estley first." Nathan excitedly jerks and ducks. "Then Estley Wood."

Steve drives.

Going through the estate the two men, stolid and still, look straight ahead. Nathan leans forward to look around at children on the pavement, blushes when he sees some friends. Laughs and sits back happily when the boys see him.

"Be worth asking Dan and Simon's mates?" Steve, slowing, asks Nathan. And Nathan could do the asking.

"Nah." Nathan shakes his head. "Dan and Simon never tell no-one what they're about." Nathan doesn't want to talk to the older boys. "I only know where they went 'cos I followed them."

"Maybe after." Martin says. "Let's suss this wall out first."

Martin looks across at Steve behind the wheel—to see if he agrees. Steve speeds up. Martin takes in the clipboards on the black dash top, the maps in the glove compartment—all arranged in Steve's order—pens in elasticated rings clipped by a magnet to the ashtray. Hanging up behind Nathan, on a stuck on plastic hook, is a blue body-warmer and an orange anorak.

Picking out maps Martin flips through them, puts them back upside down. Steve, glancing over, has watched him. No sooner is the road out among fields than they are in the dark village of Estley. The wood hangs green above it.

"Where now?" Martin asks Nathan. The question is a command to tell him the answer: no kindness in the voice. Which is not how Steve talks to Julie and Dan: he is cheerful to them, they are miserable to him.

"Well you go across here, and you go up through there." Nathan, used to being spoken to in this manner, has sat forward, "It's not these woods here. You go on up the hill. And it's the other woods."

"Here?" Steve slows on a bend, a lane going off to the right.

"No. That goes down to a farm. Yea, I think it goes to a farm. We go on up."

They are out among fields again, but climbing now.

"I had to hide here." Nathan acts ducking down.

"Watch where we're going!" Martin tells him. "Steve

doesn't want to have to reverse back to any turnings." That's the sort of thing Mary says to their children: Steve realises that Martin can't drive.

The high, unladen van sways side to side around the uphill bends.

"Just up here." Nathan points to a road forking off to the right. "Up here. Into those woods. The road goes on—on beside the wall. But they turned off before that. On their bikes. Up a track into the woods. There! That's where they went."

Steve has been driving slowly. All three look along a black churned-up bridle path as they go on past. Martin, leaning forward, squints up at the stone wall, at the razor wire coiled along the top of the wall.

The van trundles on past a high grey-white metal gate.

"Has to be a bloody gangster's wall, don't it? A gangster's bloody wall our two bright sparks go and climb over. They did climb over?" Martin asks Nathan, quickly, as if to catch him out.

"Yea. Back on that track. Go back—I'll show you."

The road past the wall has led them down to the road they left at the fork. Steve takes the van out into the road, turns it.

Going slowly back past the high metal gate, Martin says, "Don't park too close. Don't know what kind of trouble they might've got themselves into. That a lay-by back a bit?"

"Gateway," Steve says.

The square van fits slantwise into the once-gateway. Nettles and brambles have grown up through the bars of the alloy gate. Behind the gate, a leaf and grass track goes off around the inside of the wood. Fields slope away from the wood's edge—down to Estley, gathered about the road below, its slate roofs seen through gaps in Estley Wood. Away across more fields, and behind the grey moat of the motorway, are Hambrook's roofs, like a flat shale tip of red and white tiles.

Nathan and Martin have to slide across the seat to get out Steve's door. Nathan then runs ahead, skips sideways back, to lead the two slow men up the incline to the wall.

"Here." He points to the black peat path. Steve wants him to be quiet. Martin says nothing.

Horses and the big treads of a farm vehicle have torn up the mulch of the track. The boy, in his trainers, leaps lightly across the soft parts. The two men take large strides (Martin the larger) and sink. They are both careful not to bump one another. Both glance back and forth over the wall.

"It was here." Nathan says. "Yea it was here." He runs forward to look along the curving path, comes back and looks down into the wood. "Yea I hid there. That's where I watched from." He gestures with the side of his hand to a holly thicket beside a stout grey beech trunk.

Martin has walked around the nearest tree.

"Branch been cut off. Look," he tells Steve. Steve looks up at the yellow-ended stump of a thick bough. "That branch would've grown out over the wall. Look at the light coming through now."

"Fresh sawdust here," Nathan says. Sharp white and yellow granules have been sprayed across the path.

"Ladder was here," Martin squats beside two deep indentations.

"And here," Nathan says from the side.

"There's the branch," Steve says, glad to be able to contribute something. He points away from the wall.

A large bough has been cut into short sections and

rolled on top of a brown under-bristled gorse bush. Limp leaf-end trimmings have been chucked over it all.

"Reckon they knew our boys were climbing over here?" Steve looks behind himself as if being watched.

"Looks like," Martin says.

Both men leave the track and stand side by side to look up at the wall. Nathan has gone down to investigate his hiding place. Hearing him coming back, Steve says, "What you think?"

"Two things," answers Martin. "They're not here at all, or they got stuck over the other side when the branch was cut off."

"Where'd they leave their bikes?" Steve asks Nathan.

"Over there." Nathan nods his clipped head to the heap of logs and trimmings. "Was a bush there."

They all three go to investigate, pull off branches, lift logs, squat to peer under and between compressed leafage.

"No bikes here," Martin says.

"No bike tracks up there either," says Nathan. "Tracks back there though."

"Dan!" Steve shouts, surprising himself, feels his face go red, but shouts again, "Dan!"

"Simon!" Martin shouts. They take it in turn to shout. And again. They listen.

The silent woods and the wall listen back to them.

"They could've gone looking for another way out." Steve says.

"In which case why aren't they home? We're gonna have to have a look over there." Martin decides.

"They got a camera thing at the gate. Like they have in flats."

Martin nods, starts back along the track.

"Can't go in that way then," he says. "What'd we say?

You know our two. What if they been up to some mischief in there? Don't want to land 'em in it."

"Take an extension ladder to get over there though. Then you got the wire ..."

"Nah. Do it like the boys. Except you bring the van close up to the wall. On the bend this end—out of sight of the gate. I'll get on top, grab a branch, get up and over."

"Roof's only tin. Won't take your weight." Steve glances up to Martin's frown. "Nate'd be better."

"You're fuckin' jokin'. One son already lost over there I'm not going to send another. Nah, if I keep to the side of the roof, where the stanchions are, won't cause no damage."

"I'll go Dad," Nathan says.

"Need you over here." They have reached the road. "What we'll do is this. Don't want the van stuck parked out here. Soon as I'm over the wall, Steve can park the van back in the gateway. Nate you wait where I climbed over. When you hear me call you run and fetch Steve. OK?"

Steve, uneasy, goes to bring up the van. Steve doesn't like what he's doing here, and can already feel events taking him out of his depth. "If you don't do anything wrong then they can't blame you," he is always telling Dan. Who sneers at him. And here Steve is—using the van for private purposes, which he isn't supposed to do. Although, oddly, from his remarks, his boss—young Mr Sweet—expects him to. Hints as much every month when he checks the fuel bills against mileage. And when Steve says where he had to go that particular month, Mr Sweet gives him a wink and says, "Yea alright."

Reversing up the road isn't difficult, but uses up more fuel. Martin waves him to a stop where the road comes alongside the curving wall. Soon as Steve's got the back unlocked and the shutter pushed up open, Martin, using the horizontal tie-bars as steps, climbs up to the roof. The most awkward part for him is getting up over the door roller and twisting around to sit on the roof.

Sat up there, Martin then tells Steve to reverse back until a branch from over the wall comes within reach. He bangs on the roof.

Not wanting to throw Martin to the ground, Steve brakes gently. Then he has to edge forward until Martin bangs again.

Getting into and out of the van has made Steve hot. Before Steve is out of the cab this time, Martin has hoisted himself up onto the bending branch and is pulling himself along it over the top of the wall.

"Wait here," Steve tells Nathan to make sure he's understood. "Hide over there if anyone comes," pointing to the trees on the other side of the road.

"When your dad shouts come and get me." While Steve has been saying this, Nathan has looked at him with a sneer.

"Yeah, OK," he says in such a way that means he didn't need to be told what to do by this little fat man.

Although Martin prides himself on his physical strength, his arm muscles are unused to climbing—to bearing his body weight. He feels that his trembling is being transmitted to every branch end, imagines the top of the tree jigging about to his heavy movements. He hurries to cover it, which adds to his nervousness, as does the two wall-top wires passing closely below him. The outer one is coiled razor wire. The inner, a taut single strand, has little labels attached to it at intervals. Each label has a black lightning flash on a yellow background.

Reaching the solidity of the trunk, Martin pauses to catch his breath, examines this green mossier side of the

wall below him. He wonders if, trying to get out in a hurry,
one of the boys accidentally grabbed the electric wire; and
the other—going to help—caught hold of him; and so both
were electrocuted. The owner wouldn't want to advertise
the deaths. Not with his reputation. Nor pay the insurance.
Would he, though, be allowed to have a wire carrying a
charge strong enough to kill?

He hears Steve telling Nathan what to do, hears the
van drive off, and grunts a smile to hear Nate call Steve 'a
fat git'. The smile goes and he squints at his assuming that
the two boys could be dead. He despises his weakling
sneaking-around son sometimes, but he doesn't want him to
have died. No, he tells himself, he doesn't want that.

He touches the tree for luck and works his way, branch
to branch, down to the ground. His legs shaky he again
pauses, this time to listen. He looks along the wall path in
both directions, peers down into the woods, can hear only
the repetitive cooing of a dove, see only foliage beyond dark
green foliage.

Having made a line with his heel through the leaf-
mould of the path, so he'll know which tree was his,
glancing always into the wood, Martin creeps around this
darker side of the wall—away from the gate and towards
Dan and Simon's crossing point.

At a break in the trees he makes out the grey roof
corner of the house, part of a black window below it. Martin
looks at it and hates the occupant of that house. Not
because he thinks the owner is an unpunished gangster, but
simply because to be the owner of the house he has to be
rich. Doesn't matter to Martin how the rich come by their
money, once rich they're the same the world over—smug
and contemptuous, fat and undeserving of his sympathy.

The poor are different, Martin believes, different from

each other. The poor have to adapt to each of their hard circumstances, take their shapes from that.

Through another gap in the leafage Martin makes out the white point of a lake. His second sight of it stops him. Among the trees, in the blue air held over the lake, is a palpable stillness, like the high singing note sustained by a circular saw.

Martin, trying to make even less noise, creeps on. He knows—by the gap in the leaf canopy—that he has reached the crossing place. On this side too a big branch has been cut down. Ladder marks on the ground here too, and a domed bed of sawdust where the branch was sectioned. But, on this side, there's no stack of timber, only a circle of ash from a recent fire.

Martin stands looking down at the grey and white pyramid of ash. Why would anyone go to the trouble of burning green wood?

"Simon!" he hears himself call low. "Simon!"

He can hear no response, no-one coming.

"Simon!" he listens. "Dan!" A bird takes clattering flight. "Dan!"

In the far distance a car blares its horn. Looking down at the ash Martin is aware of a sick frightened feeling deep in his gut. He doesn't want to be afraid. He doesn't like the idea of himself being afraid.

A whirring noise has him raise his head: a large yellow-green dragonfly circles around him. Its transparent wings click together like loose tappits. So close does it come that Martin can see that its long body is made, apparently, of red and black cones stuck one into the end of another.

When the dragonfly perches on a dock leaf Martin leans close, sees that on the tip of each of its four wings is a black spot. The head is comprised mostly of mouth and sectioned eyes. Has it come to watch him?

When he moves forward for a closer look the dragonfly, with a rattle, rises vertically. Looking up Martin can see its green deep-chested thorax, muscles for wings and legs. A living thing, not artificial. It whirrs off towards the lake.

Without having made the decision Martin finds himself hurrying back along the darkening path by the wall. He finds his line.

"Nate!" he calls low. What if this son too doesn't answer? "Nate!"

"Dad?" comes the stage whisper.

"Get the van."

Martin takes his time climbing the tree, edges out along the branch, sees the van—with flush-faced Nathan sat in the back—reversing along. Nathan bangs with the flat of his hand when they're underneath. Martin lets himself hang, doesn't release the branch till his backside is on the roof, which dents with a boink when he lets go.

Shuffling around, lying flat, body bent in half, he finds footholds on the tie-rails.

"Not there?" Steve says when Martin reaches the van floor.

"No." Martin pulls down the squeal-echoing roller door. "Let's get outa here."

The three of them squash into the front of the van.

"What's up?" Steve says as they drive away. Martin eases a muscle in his back,

"Dunno. But there's a bonfire on the other side. Why'd he make a bonfire of green wood?"

"Ah ..." Steve's plump-wristed hand waves that idea away, "The little buggers have gone off somewhere else."

"Where?" Martin asks him.

# 9

Coming back up the drive today—I must tell you this sister,
there's no-one else—coming back up the drive, a greater-
spotted woodpecker flew just ahead of the car. And on every
dip that it took, its black and white tail-feathers were fanned
out. Each tail-feather was red-tipped.

It was exhilarating. Especially as I'd been listening all
afternoon to a man telling of how he misses his wife. The
little things. Who, for instance, does he go on holiday with
now? Or just for a weekend drive? For a local walk? "I'm a
prisoner inside my loneliness," he said. And for a moment I
saw the walls around this garden in that light. But not so
sister, they're to keep danger out.

I know what he meant though sister. I know; and
writing this I look, now, for somewhere in the past on whom
to lay the blame for this cruel gift—for my being able to
understand his pain. And it's all down to you sister. Why all
of my life I've been alone. And I've known I've been alone
because you should have been there with me.

You should have been there with me when I started
school. I was alone. For every one of my life's events you
should have been there, my companion and measure. And I
was alone. Or entrusted to the care of strangers; and those
strangers could not care because they were not a part of me
and I was not a part of them. My life and their life could be
separated by them at any time they chose. No morphic field
to bind us: mine was a name to be forgotten.

No-one could have taken your part sister. Only you. And, until I made you inside me, I was alone.

We are all damaged people, sister—none of us perfect. We are all the victims of our parents and to blame for our children. So it goes on. But where I am often puzzled by my children's contrary behaviour (merely puzzled), I am offended by our parents'. Because our parents continue to be a resented part of me; and my children are not shaping me, but me them. Poor dears.

I, we, had parents both of whom had the attitude that nothing in their child's life—friendships, loves, enmities, passions—could be so important as that in their own. What happened to blind our mother that she didn't see what was happening to me?

I've looked for clues in old family photographs, of times before I was born. And I see in part of a face—a hairline, or jaw—a piece of my photographed own. And seeing that part of a face in a woman, in a girl, I see you. So, inside me, you are dressed always in the fashions of the past.

Our mother has told me that she was criticised as a child, rarely praised. So, like all those with low self-esteem, she sought fame. And, having achieved that fame, she is dismissive of it. She calls it illusory, superficial, ephemeral; because she is still of low self-esteem and so, if she can own it—then, low self-esteem intact—fame isn't worth having. The attention and praise was worth it though; and to get that took time, sister, took her away from me.

No nanny helped. If any nanny saw what was wrong with me—loneliness—they only used it to score points over my neglectful parents, their exploitive employers. Same for every set of teachers. Wherever I got moved.

It was in the moves, sister, that you grew inside me. It was all the moving back then that makes this place so important now. It is not moving that makes this place so dangerous. Here I am a stationary target.

Let me explain to you about our loving parents, sister, about our family of four—three living, one dead—a public/private family unit.

The private family unit, sister, is the world's oldest torture chamber. And we're all of us born into one. So let me tell you about our very public family unit. Let me tell you about their very public marriage and divorce. Let me tell you how that, when your parents' marriage is a subject of public speculation, the child of that marriage has few places to be himself. I went inside me to you, sister.

Textbooks say that, in memory, childhood becomes a permanent place, becomes set in perspex, all traumatic change being stilled to notable moments. My memories of my childhood are all of movement, traumatic movement.

Of course I got into trouble at school.

Most children are taught to believe that everything makes sense, if only examined and the appropriate rules and laws applied. Then those taught children meet with Life itself, their participant/spectator role in it; and there is confusion of cause and effect, debate over beginnings and ends; and those grown children are outraged over the uncertainty.

Sister, I was schooled in uncertainty. At every new school I had to learn the new rules. Teachers always assumed that I knew those rules. Or, condescendingly, used me as an example, "Here we don't behave in that manner." Do you know why injustice in schooldays rankles more than in later life? It is because as a child you, literally, know no better. Every unjust accusation therefore is Innocence, is Trust, betrayed.

I learnt to judge the rules. While watching other

newcomers—we are a world of people in flux sister Clare—
blindly obey the new rules. I saw then that most people,
both children and adults, want only to learn the rules of any
new situation; and then, abiding by the rules, belong to that
situation. Thus do most people get to be guards at
concentration camps. I didn't follow rules, got to do my
own killing.

Although schools figure large in each our memories,
we figure small in theirs. And, outside of class, at every new
school I had to prove myself.

The closest some children get to physical contact is
fighting someone. And the absent parents, and the teachers
at their remove, wonder why the child so enjoys fighting.

That's how it begins anyway. Then it gets to be about
winning, about inflicting pain, about having power. Later
still it gets to be with the self-hating morals of a drunk.
"Why do you need to fight?" our father, the deepening-his-
voice actor, asked me. Every day on the telly were war films,
martial art films, cop films, series (he'd starred in a few of
them, had fought to get the parts), and they all contained
the same old message—let's admire the warrior. Why did I
need to fight? Participating fool!

School curricula varied. At every school I was put into
a lower set. Reports of my 'attitude' preceded me.
Consequently it confused my teachers that I enjoyed
learning: I didn't fit their textbook 'challenging behaviour'.

I had to fight to be me, fight to own my own
experience and therefore my identity. Learning was a
weapon in that fight.

I knew then that we all have incomplete educations,
have therefore to act on imperfect understandings. How do
we build ourselves, I used to wonder. We can, we do, we do
what we can, but each and every of our buildings is flawed. I

could not make myself perfect.

Learning was certainly not something that I wanted to show off. But, so that I couldn't be patronised by the agents and actors who crept around our hot-property mother, I had to know what they were talking about so that I could sneer back at them. (She tried to applaud me the first couple of times, stopped when I rounded on her.)

Of course I got into trouble with authority. Of course I stole from our parents. Our mother was more puzzled than offended. As I am puzzled by Marilyn and Ollie's unforgivingness.

I tell myself that I don't mind Ollie and Mal using me. It is after all a parent's function to be used by their children. The degree to which they are used is up to the parent—I give mine money, would give them time too if they'd let me. (It is to pervert chronology for the parent to make use of the child. Which is another reason why sexual abuse is so instinctively abhorrent.) "We didn't abuse you." our mother said. As if absence of abuse was proof of love. And it is true that I wasn't, according to any textbook definition, neglected. Our mother dutifully made time for me in her schedule, was a good and conscientious mother in her own eyes.

Not in mine. I sensed a hollowness, a lack of genuine affection. And sensing that falsity I early became estranged, incapable of being reached by her. To the tearful puzzlement of our mother who truly felt that she had done everything right, had followed all the rules.

I hadn't wanted her though to make us—dead you, live me—a cause celebre, innocuous as a rare illness, something to be wrapped in sentimentality on one chat show after another. So it was that my later aberrant behaviour, my deliberated wrongdoing, had to be too dangerous for her to mention. In her scale of things it could not even aspire to infamy, lest it, lest I become another public 'problem'.

I'm sick of talking of them. Whoever our parents are they leave us a legacy of unsociable gratitudes and grievances. I'm over-endowed with anger. And I'm sick of them. I will not, sister, accept them.

As soon as I'd made it impossible for them to accept me I walked out on them.

# 10

Caught up in the adventure—he has seen his father this day climb red-to-purple faced up into and out of trees—as soon as the van stops Nathan jumps down and goes running to fetch his mother.

Martin gets out more slowly, goes to the back of the van to direct Steve into the drive. He knows that Steve doesn't need his help, but doesn't want to be sat there in the cab looking stupidly forward while the van goes backwards.

Steve takes more care than usual reversing—to take his time, to put off the moment. He is aware of Mary waiting just inside the open door, a back-and-forth rocking in her stance.

Martin, embarrassed by her undisguised anxiety, says, as if to himself,

"Where's Nate got to?" and he looks down the street.

Mary looks uncomprehending across at Martin. She makes no attempt to speak, waits for Steve to get out of the van before stepping out of the door and saying,

"Where's Dan? Where is he?"

Steve looks down at the freckled hand gripping his sleeve, up into her fixed blue eyes.

"Don't know." He pats the back of her hand, offers an apologetic smile.

"Nate's gone for Tina." Martin loudly tells her. "We'll all have a talk." He glances up and down the street. "Decide what best to do."

Tina appears—hurrying with Nathan, her head tilted half-listening to Nathan's gasping chatter. Tina has on a fawn cardigan over her striped supermarket tunic.

"Let's go in." Steve says.

His sleeve is still gripped in Mary's fist. The family across the way have stood up from their television to look out the window.

"Come on." Steve tries to turn Mary; but she is stuck watching Tina walk towards them.

The only time Mary knows Tina from before is when Daniel and Simon crashed the car they stole. Tina shouted her mouth off in the court buildings and Mary tried not to be seen with her.

"Hello Mary." Tina wriggles her bum between the van and the brick gate pillar. "Children eh? Who'd have 'em?"

Mary releases her hold on Steve's sleeve, transfers it to Tina's cardigan,

"Where are they?"

"Probably somewhere stupid and obvious. Looking us in the face. Let's go inside Mary." Tina looks with apparent fierceness in turn at the two men. "Little bastards worrying us again like this."

Since a child Tina has prided herself on being hard. Chose a hard man to marry. Is hard on her boys. Hard to the world. Hard about every aspect of life—birth, procreation and death. Hard.

Tina's father, here in Hambrook, was a drunken bully. Loud he was, coarse, and damaging. Tina learnt, before she can remember, to shout at him when he was hungover. At her mother too—for wearing her bruises out in public, like she was proud of the brutality handed out to her.

Tina is more than hard now. Harder than hard now. Because Tina knows, with a certainty beyond logic, that something terrible, something unspeakable to the mother, has happened to her flesh-and-blood son. Otherwise he would be home.

Martin can pretend to himself that he doesn't know, but she has gone numb inside. And—hard outside, numb inside—she knows that it doesn't matter what she does now, it will not help her son. He has gone beyond help, his fate already happened. It doesn't matter what she does, so she has brought herself along here to the Flinthorns, going numbly along with the logic of the situation.

Steve, nervously nodding and fat man grimacing, leads the way indoors, shows Martin and Tina into the living room. Nathan, curious about the stress pulled tight over Mary's face, watching her, comes behind.

Tina nudges Martin to sit on the sofa. Steve turns the armchair so that it's facing them. Mary, though, won't come and sit in it, has stopped at the door,

"Where are they?"

Nathan slips past Mary to half-sit on the edge of the sofa.

"Short answer," Martin edges forward to look around Nathan at Mary, "is we don't know."

"Nate says they cut the branches off where they went over." Tina prods Martin's leg to make him look at her. "Nate says they've got trapped in there."

"Yea." He sits back. "Could be."

"If they got trapped in there then how come you got out?"

"I dropped onto the top of the van."

"Why couldn't they get out?"

Steve, feeling sorry for Martin in face of this unsympathetic questioning, tells her,

"Long drop to the ground. Doubt they could do it.

And not break a leg."

"They not got a gate there?" Tina sarcastically asks Steve.

"Yea. Yea they have," Steve blushes, "but it's as high as the wall. They couldn't have got out through that."

"Neither of 'em are totally stupid." Tina says. "Why haven't they asked to be let out?"

"Know who the owner is?" Martin asks her.

"Yea. That gangster. You said."

Mary lets out a little groan, comes crouching to sit in the armchair.

"We don't know they're there for sure." Steve pats her shoulder.

"Nor do we know, if they are there, they've come to any harm." Martin looks across at her, "I was thinking—on the way back down—you know what a couple of sods our two are—what if he's recruited them? What if he's caught them, and now he's got them working for him?"

"Dan would've let us know." Mary says. "He would've let us know."

No-one in the room believes her. Steve's light squeeze on her shoulder reminds her that Dan bunked off school for weeks on end without telling them.

Julie comes banging down the stairs and into the silent room.

"Can't find any tights," she accuses her mother.

"I washed some ..." Mary pulls herself out of her worry, "Yesterday?"

"Can't find any."

"Your brother's missing." Steve tells her, his hand holding Mary in the chair.

Julie looks down at skinny Nathan, tubby Tina and dour Martin.

"He'll turn up," she says. "Bad news always does. Where's my tights?" Her legs are shaven white. "I gotta go."

"Out the back!" Mary's remembering is almost a shout. "They'll be dry."

Having been able to pander to her rude daughter Mary sits back, for the moment, relieved, her guilt assuaged. The guilt being why she allows her daughter and son to be so rude to her. Guilt for felt neglect of them both—while she and Steve have been off enjoying themselves.

Steve had a mini when he first started going out with Mary. They used to have sex in it, beside it, once on it. They used to have sex everywhere. Couldn't stop touching one another. Even after the children were born. Whole of their married life it has been their one huge chuckling secret.

Julie lets the back door bang behind her.

"What if," Martin says, "they been told not to tell us?"

"They'd be too full of themselves." Tina enters into the spirit of Martin's argument. "I reckon, if like you say he's caught 'em, he's got 'em locked up somewhere."

"They might not," Mary's every word sounds like it's being pressed out of her, "might not be there at all."

"Coincidence if they're not." Martin says. "Last seen climbing this one tree to get over the wall. That tree's now had its branches cut off. Why else would the branches been cut off?"

"Tell the police." Mary says.

"Dodgy." Martin shakes his head.

From the sofa's arm Nathan, bored by all this talk now, watches his father try to win this stupidly worried woman over to his way of thinking. Yet this is the house where Dan did his growing up. With these two dumpy people.

"I agree with you—something has definitely happened to them." Martin says. "We got to assume though that both boys are still alive. And if they're still alive, then they're either staying there of their own free will, or he's got them prisoners. So, either way, what's going to happen to them if we get the police involved? If they're there voluntarily then they're going to be in trouble both with the law and with their new boss. And if they're being held against their will... well he might just decide that they're not worth the bother, and get rid of the two of them. We got to act careful."

"So what you gonna do?" Tina asks him, superior in her certainty, wanting now only to put the others at their ease, to let Martin find out his own way, in his own time. She feels protective towards him, knows that he won't know how to deal with this loss, who to blame. "So what you gonna do?" she asks him again. "Just leave our sons there? What if they're not there?"

"Why would they stay there?" Mary's question is a cry. "Why? If they didn't have to. Don't be daft," she tails off.

"He could be paying them." Martin says quietly, almost kindly. "And not just in money either. What if he's got a couple of women in for them? Know what lads are like at that age, always whanging their meat. Probably up there now shagging themselves silly. While we're down here worrying."

Nathan's grin is hidden from his father's glance.

"Tell you what," Martin continues, "Steve and I'll go back up tomorrow after work. I'll have a look at the house. See if they're being kept in there. And I'll have a look-see if there's any other buildings they might be hiding in. Sheds and that. It's a huge place."

"I'll come." Nathan says. "I can get over."

"No you don't." Tina says. "One son missing's

enough—thank you very much."

"What if they're not there?" Mary's shriek of anxiety cuts through the room. "What if they're not? We gotta tell the police." She sobs out once, holds it back.

"Could be the worse thing we do love." Steve bends over the back of the armchair to tell her. "Police are probably already in his pocket. Got to be. Everybody knows he's a gangster. But he still goes on living up there. The police go on letting him live up there. We got to go careful."

"They could be somewhere else." Tina tells Steve.

"If they're not there tomorrow," Steve says to Martin, "and they haven't turned up, then we'll go to the police. Agreed?"

None disagree.

Steve lets go Mary's shoulder.

"I gotta push that bump out of the van's roof."

"I'll give you a hand." Martin gets up to go with him.

# 11

To the willow
all hatred, and desire
of your heart.

**Basho** (1644-1694)

OK sister, how did I become a gangster?

Contempt, I guess. Contempt for everyone I knew, contempt for every value they held.

As a child you are told that all adults know better than you. By the time you get through your teens, however, you realise that there's no adult solidarity—all blame each other. And they'll blame you if you give them half a chance. Blame you for the shitty state of their lives. Anything they can pin on you. Might just as well, then, give them cause to blame you.

That's the state of mind.

How did it actually start?

Wasn't a conscious decision. It grew. It evolved.

Most gangsters start off wanting to be rich. Or they want to lord it over their neighbourhood. I was already rich; and I had already moved around so much that I didn't have a neighbourhood. I wanted, anyway, more than that. Or something other.

Was it a greed for power? For recognition? For fame like our parents? For another kind of fame?

Nothing so identifiable back then. Back then I just hated everyone.

Another consideration—how much, when young, are human beings driven by curiosity as much as desire? Can the two be separated? As we get older, is it not desire that diminishes, but curiosity which is sated? What think you sister?

Forget right and wrong sister, and look at the parameters within which 'decent' people exist. The policeman who commits, out of frustration, a single brutal act. Or the legitimate protester who, also out of frustration, smashes a window. Both are conscience-stricken. (I've met them, have listened in amazement.) What does their being decent depend on? On having a thought for other people? Or on having a thought for what other people might think of them? Or is it out of a desire to be doing the right thing, or a religious wish not to hurt people like themselves—not to damage the image of themselves as decent people?

When it came to killing, mine wasn't the usual cowardice, common to all creatures, of attacking the smaller and weaker; or the cowardice of creatures defending their young only to the point where it endangers their own existence. Heroism—of the sort where the hero sacrifices himself—is a human corporate invention. My contempt was for everyone, including myself—therefore I put myself in danger.

Towards the end of my schooldays I was feared. I was unorthodox, abnormal, unpredictable. I carried a gun, but not for defence, nor did I fantasise about having to use it. I took the pistol to school, pressed it against a boy's ear and forced him to kiss me. To kiss you. He had floppy blond hair. I made him work his lips.

For me it was an important experiment. For him it was

a private humiliation.

Teachers, by teacher intuition, knew I was trouble. My 'defiance' often got them into trouble. One teacher sussed me out. "How can you think so little of yourself that what you do in life doesn't matter? You do matter. Believe that, or die young. You matter."

He was right. I knew he was right: I did matter. But only to myself as myself: I had an underlying conceit. And that conceit wouldn't let me do anything less than the absolute best. But I had, then, yet to pick what I wanted to excel in.

I already knew that I could be anything I wanted, that every hero and every monster lived within me. I also knew that men—men as tribe, men as society—must have a system, a code to live by; else they fuck and kill everything in sight.

I was no exception. I too needed a system, and didn't want to fuck and kill everything. I just hadn't found a worthwhile code. What made me different from most men, however, was that—whereas most men don't look beyond what's on offer, and have to have the rules made for them—I was conceited enough to make my own.

One would-be gangster, still at school, not too intelligent, loudly built himself up to approach me—the idea being, I suppose, to take some of our parents' money off me. (They were famous, therefore they were rich, he reasoned.) I shot him in the foot, and told him that if anyone was told, I'd put a bullet up his nose.

He was already in the employ of a local villain. That local villain recruited me. As a test of fitness, I was sent to frighten another gang.

It was the usual inner-city gang rivalry—territories, areas of influence, the control of pimps, protection, dealerships, percentages. A subculture as hard to get into as the civil service.

I was taken to be shown the other gang, whose members actually wore a kind of uniform—black rayon jackets—so they were easily identified.

Never trust a reputation, sister. That gang did. I had this other nervous new gang member with me. "What d'you think we should do?" he kept asking me. Got on my nerves. "What d'you think we should do?"

I told him to wait and watch. And, in a crowded street, I walked up behind two black rayon jackets and shot them both in the back of the head. So quick was I, that even the second one hadn't known what had hit him. And I'd walked down an alley, was around a corner, before the first scream. (In any crowd, some woman, seeing blood, will scream. Would you have screamed, sister? Or would you, like me, have stood back and watched the play?)

Ultimately, sister, every new decision is a snap decision. I hadn't known what I was going to do before I saw them walking along together, full of their own wrong power.

Acting on such an impulse was exhilarating. But real, because of the danger. It was not sanitised television violence—how I hated Mal and Ollie watching that—excitement without the fear. My own death, end-of-the-life-I-knew, was on that street.

Those two killings scared the shit out of the black rayon gang, but also out of the gang who'd recruited me. (Before meeting them, I always expect my social superiors to be wise. Always, after only a few tell-tale moments in their company, I am disappointed.) That gang leader's naked fear disappointed me—his worry more than his fear. Warriors shouldn't have worries.

That leader, who in ordinary circumstances had the loud self-assurance of most big men, after the killings was all for going to ground—in case the black rayons tried for a revenge killing. I told him to get a message to his black rayon counterpart saying, as if they'd attacked one of ours, that if any more of ours were attacked, it'd be three of theirs next time. "You'll do that?" he asked me. "Course," I told him.

One of his blokes was hit in a drive-by. Not killed. It then took me all day, calling around at their houses, to kill the three I'd promised. (The odd thing was, because they relied on reputation—were following rules spoken and unspoken—the black rayons had places and times they thought they were immune from attack. I know I'm not immune here, sister. I knew that I was not immune when they killed Fay, Darren and baby Bonny. My oversight. My miscalculation. My complacency.)

Could you have killed anyone, sister? It's easy enough. Once you've fitted it into a value system. Like any soldier. Or once you've questioned the sanctity of life, the mythology of the sanctity of life. We die. Who notices? Who cares? This life, this here and now, is always temporary.

Once those conclusions are reached, killing bears no more thinking about than washing a car. Their life stops. Their past—all their memories—the whole of that stops. Their future—hopes and dreams—that stops too. Their life, their breath upon breath reality, is gone. Your reality, your life, now contains their death. You go on.

After every killing, as you know sister, I went to look for a fuck. Fucking—with a hard-on that won't go away— that fucking and fucking and fucking was, I believe, an affirmation of life. I don't think Fay ever realised where those sudden needs for her came from. No, I'm sure she didn't; it would have frightened her to have known.

Back then, after those three killings, our boss was terrified of a counter-attack. I got him to drop a rumour to the police that the killings were the consequence of a power struggle within the black rayons. And the black rayons were so fired up by this time, and so indiscreet—armed to the teeth—that they dropped themselves in it. The police did our work for us.

I was put on the payroll. The hierarchy of the gang, though, saw me as a threat. (I did not try to be like them. I did not try to be liked by them.) One tried to pull rank on me. I shot him in the face.

Because I hadn't talked first, and had let the gun do the talking for me, the others backed off. I already knew from school, from every new school, not to threaten or promise what I was incapable of delivering—just to act, and then to let them come to terms with that fact.

In that first gang I was put to work running a string of pimps, dealing with ambitious dealers, sorting out late-payers ... all the usual inner-city stuff.

I was more intelligent than most, and could see how many gangsters set themselves up to fail. It mattered to them being a gangster; they had, therefore, to be seen being a gangster. So they dressed like a gangster, and used gangster slang. (Slang, sister, is the language of the inarticulate.)

Criminals should not advertise. For my part, I just saw crime as a way of making a lot of money, independently from our parents.

Prior to meeting, to talking, most young men look like thugs to one another. I washed my hair a lot, and looked like a sharp young American. Seen as successful by my gangster contemporaries, I was copied. Success creates problems: one can appear to be copying oneself.

As for the work, intimidation has its own techniques. Bluff doesn't work—not for long. I used to carry a silver thermos of hot water and pour it over recalcitrant's hands. So, if someone came to me wearing gloves, I knew I was in for a fight.

I learnt to recognise other danger signs. People pushed beyond the limit are like dynamite, when it starts to sweat. Then, one touch, and—BANG!

I knew, of course, that once I had started, there'd be no escape from gangsterism—that to survive I had to become part of the gangster establishment. This meant only that I was one remove from physical action. I did not want to become 'respectable'.

I span my boss a tale off the top of my head one day— just to keep his ears busy—a semi-plausible scheme of this and that, a means maybe to make more money, just an idea. Then, afterwards, I thought "Why not?" And so I made the money, for myself.

The only restrictions on a gangster are those he imposes on himself.

Having built up a nest egg, I started to fund robberies and big dope deals—taking my cut, of course. Speculate to accumulate. And I moved out of the territory—no longer wanted to be associated with it, hampered by it.

One gang I financed welshed on me. I killed them all, one by one, kept their bodies in a rented deep freeze, then burnt them in a van on top of a hill. Not as vengeance, you understand, sister—vengeance gives only a little bit of satisfaction—but as a warning to others.

(In case you're worried, sister, these letters to you are in code, are in our twin language that we never fully developed. Was it in the womb there, in our breathed amniotic fluid, waiting for us to use it? Using it here at last definitely feels good—it's a release, talking to you sister like this. Putting into these odd words what before I only told you in my mind.)

Do you think I'm mad, sister? No madder than my time, I think. To survive, I've had to accommodate to the madnesses of others, to assimilate their madnesses into the logic of myself.

Understand that this is not shame, I'm unburdening here. Just things, of necessity, that I had to keep to myself. (And we all of us know things about ourselves that no-one else knows—toilet habits, sexual fantasies, tiny betrayals ... Some of us have voices talking to us. They're not secrets, nor symptoms of insanity, just the inner speaking of our own knowledge.)

Back to my story.

My original boss actually died of a heroin overdose. Not my doing. His own. And I simply stepped into his place—no-one was going to stop me—and carried on with my funding, and let my second-in-command run the pimps and the dealers.

He was good at what he did: it was our concept of the scale of things that made us different. Small-time villains— my second-in-commands—were pursued by small-time police. The large scale villainy I was aiming for, and got, was the province of national police forces. (The machinery of institutions is indifferent to any individual's separate existence. The machinery is a code to be followed—or broken.)

Eventually, having built up a decent and legal investment portfolio, I left the villains to it. And I came here in semi-retirement.

My villainous past is rumoured locally. Which is why, I reckon, I make such a good Acceptor. Believing me capable of anything, people feel they can tell me anything.

Mind you, sister, the nice professional people I work with now, although—for a thrill—they may whisper my reputation, they have no concept of its reality, nor of its savagery.

Some of the clients are shocked when they realise who I am. A few get a bit too curious. Most, though, are wholly concerned about their own, failed selves. And, even if they're not, by then they're usually too deep in to withdraw.

# 12

As agreed, after dinner—which should have given Mr Sweet plenty of time to get home, to not see the van being used—Steve stops outside Martin's house.

Martin comes striding out as soon as the van stops—he was looking out for it.

"Open the back," he tells Steve, and he goes off to his workshop.

This unexpected instruction upsets Steve: it means he has to turn the engine off and take the keys round the back for the padlock.

Hambrook is full of people who know what's right for other people. They know, looking over their hedges, out their windows, when people are up to no good. He and Martin don't look relaxed.

Martin comes out carrying an aluminium extension ladder. He slides it along the wooden floor of the van.

"Got a board too," he tells Steve, and he goes back to his workshop.

Waiting for him, Steve begins to feel easier—seeing the ladder watchers will now think he and Martin are off to do a bit of on-the-side decorating. Not that remarkable around here.

Having slid the board in, Steve pulls the shutter down. Both slam into the cab and leave.

Martin sees that the maps have been put back the way they were.

"Got a map of this area?" Martin asks.

"Only roads." Steve glances across. "Nothing large scale." But Martin has already pulled out three of the maps and begun flicking through them.

Martin chucks the maps down on the seat between them, and tells Steve what he wants to do.

"Been thinking on it all last night, all today. What I'll do is go over the wall—like I did yesterday—from the top of the van. Which is why I brought the board—save denting the roof."

Steve, listening and nodding, resents his life being taken over by this loud, unsmiling man. "Who's he think he is?" pops into Steve's head. Tonight was his darts night. Won't get there now.

He has to stop in the narrow road just above Estley, waiting for a four-wheel drive to pass. A woman is behind the steering wheel, children with her in the car. She expertly reverses back and lets Steve squeeze past. Photographs in the paper showed a wife and children who were blown up in a car like that.

"Fast as I can," Martin says, "I'm going to search right round that wood. Sheds, chalets, things like that. If they're not in any of them, then I'll get as close to the house as I can."

"He got bodyguards?"

"Didn't see any last night."

"Came back this way from a delivery today," Steve says as they are climbing the hill. "Couldn't see any sign of life. Maybe they're away."

"Could be." Martin sits forward as they enter the woods. "And I wouldn't put it past our two silly sods to go and set up house in his gaffe while he's away. Not knowing who he is."

"Could've been our two who cut off the branches."

Steve thought of that in the middle of last night. He couldn't help blaming his son for whatever has befallen him, and yet he feels guilty for wanting to blame him. Martin, though, doesn't think much of the idea, just looks at Steve as if he's said something so far-fetched it's not worth commenting on.

Steve decides he doesn't like this big bossy man into whose company his son has forced him. All of what they are about to do feels stupid and dangerous. And it is all Dan's fault.

"Pull over here. Hard against the wall." Martin tells him.

The evening sun is shining orange across the top of the wall.

"Come on," Martin hurries him.

The slatted door-roller squeaks.

"Can't you get that fucker oiled?" Martin says. Steve notices that Martin's hands are trembling as he pushes the ladder up to rest against the back of the van.

Steve has pulled out the board. Martin pauses, leans to the side to look in around the back of the van, into the corner at the tied-back stack of folded blankets.

"Don't suppose you got a set of tools on board?" he is whispering now.

"Screwdriver and hammer," Steve says. "Why?"

"If they're locked in anywhere I might need to get it open."

Steve walks slowly along to the cab, his legs reluctant to get involved in any breaking-in. But he can see no way—here and now, in the logic of their situation—he can get out of it. He pulls a rag-wrapped staple gun, a wooden-handled hammer, and a yellow-handled screwdriver out from under the seat.

Martin takes only the screwdriver, sticks it in his back pocket, and climbs up the ladder with the board under one arm. Steve stands his weight on the bottom rung of the ladder. Martin slides the board onto the roof of the van, steps up onto it, walks to a branch and tests his grips.

"Hold on," Steve comes bumping up the ladder. "One thing you've not thought of—I can't just wait here. Like this. And Nathan's not here. How'm I going to know when you want to get back?"

Steve's saying 'Nathan' and not 'Nate' irritates Martin: this fat little fucker thinks, 'cos he's out in the van all day, he's better than them on the factory floor.

"Obvious innit. You'll have to park the van down the road, come back and wait until I give you a shout. Then you'll have to go back and fetch the van."

Martin crawls more than climbs up into the bending branch. Bits of leaves and twig-ends fall down after him.

"We don't have too long," Steve stage-whispers, he pulls the board—scraping it—off the roof, and carries it wobbling down the ladder.

After stowing the board and ladder in the back, and pulling the squealing van door closed, Steve looks around for something to mark the spot where Martin went over. He could leave a stick lying in the road. A car, though, could knock that aside. He needs something more permanent. Something that will show: already, in the shadow of the wall, dusk is making distance unreliable.

"Got it!" Steve says to himself. He goes behind the passenger seat, takes out an aerosol of white paint that he uses to cover any scrapes or scratches on the van; and, so he'll be able to see it from the driver's side, he sprays a white line on the side of the road opposite the wall.

Feeling good for having done something of his own accord, Steve gets into the van and reverses back to the same gateway as yesterday.

When Martin doesn't hear the van leave—he has heel-raked his mark across the path—he gets furiously impatient, and thinks why doesn't that fat twat Steve Flinthorn leave. He is about to shout out angrily when he thinks maybe there is something happening on the other side of the wall. He thinks he hears Steve, or someone, moving about on the road, but there are no voices. Then, with an empty trundling sound, the van whines away in reverse.

Martin immediately sets off at a trot along the path beside the wall. The yellow handle of the screwdriver bumps against the bone of his hip. Thinking the screwdriver may work its way out from his back pocket Martin removes it and runs with it in his hand—like a knife, a tomahawk, a carbine.

At a break in the trees, Martin pauses to look across at the grey and silver stone house. Some small sunset clouds, up among the pink, hang like torn scraps of gold tissue paper.

The blue of evening is gathering in among the trees. It therefore must be dark indoors too, Martin thinks, but no lights are on in the house.

At the break in the trees is a path running down towards the lake. With his long backbone curved, Martin skitters down the path at a run.

Martin hasn't run like this for years. Reminds him of being a boy—that lighter-than-air pleasure of flying from one foot to the other, a whole world under each bouncing footspring.

His father wouldn't approve of him being here. There again, Martin's father approves of very little. Tall and thin, he's still worried about his mortgage, his insurance, his garden, his neighbours ... Nor would Martin's mother approve of him being here. His mother tells him she is ashamed of him. His mother is a purse-mouthed snob. His mother despises people who live in council houses.

When he was a boy, the pair of them had been hard for him to fathom—they had only prejudices, rather than a system of values. Smiling, he wonders what their prejudices would make of his running through this rich man's private property.

The downhill path has brought Martin to a clearing. He crouches, listens to his own breath, the bump-bump-bump of his heart. A treetop bird keeps up a monotonous cheep-cheep. Martin can see no sheds, no outbuildings—just the white-gold gleam of the lake.

The boys, messing about, could have fallen in the water; one getting into difficulties, one going to help the other, both drowning, the bodies floating up like white crosses ... Who'd find them here? And who, he asks as his legs are about to take him down to the water's edge, would cut off the branches and remove their bikes?

The openness around the lakeside makes him feel vulnerable. So he cuts back up into the woods, and goes jogging along a path that seems to be midway between the wall and the lake.

He passes through two more clearings. At a third, his legs have lost their spring and his lungs ache for air. And still he has glimpsed not one shed, not one outbuilding.

Stumbling on weak legs to the lower edge of this latest clearing, he leans stiff-armed against a tree and looks down at the lake. He is close to the house now. To one side is a small upside-down boat, with white scratches on its dark blue hull.

Martin can see no-one behind the cloud reflections on the windows. At the bottom end of the house are a pair of double doors. They can't, Martin thinks, be the doors for a garage, as there is no road in front of them. Must be where the boat was once kept, he decides. He decides also that that must be where the boys are being held, and he imagines himself bursting the doors apart to rescue a wide-eyed Dan and Simon—how he will be, for once, a hero to his son—at least a bigger hero than the friend who got him into this mess.

His breath gathered, the hero Martin Thurlow pushes himself back in among the trees. A jay goes, pink and blue, twisting in among the branches. It makes no noise. Martin makes no noise.

Closer to the house, this path is more worn than the others, wider too. Without being conscious of doing so, Martin has slowed to a wary walk, his eyes on the stone side of the house rising above him. In this light, behind the black leaves of the trees, its stones look pink.

On the side wall, near the sloping ground, is one round window. All the others are square and on the upper floor. Before he gets to the open ground around the house, Martin picks his way up through undergrowth of bramble and holly to get a view of the land side of the house.

No cars are parked on the rough stone road. He hears no sound, bar the same cheep-cheeping bird.

Martin plunges suddenly, runs down across the rough bit of ground, and slips—clinging to the stone wall. He has banged his knee and grimaces back the pain.

"You owe me, boy," he murmurs, releasing it. "You daft pair of bastards."

All that he can hear now is the bellow-hammer of his own lungs and heart.

On his backside he scuttles down to the corner of the house, and gets on his knees to look around it. A concrete path runs along in front of a line of recessed, full-length windows. The double doors to the boat-house are at the far end.

Again Martin takes a breath and a plunge, and steps upright into full view before the first window.

Behind the double-glazing is a stairwell—stairs going up beside the round window in the wall, a hall of oak floorboards leading back into the house. No-one there.

Two paces brings him in front of the next long window. Its wooden frame, probably pine, is stained a mahogany-pink. Martin shades his face to look through his double-edged silhouette. Inside is a bedroom, thick carpet, fitted wardrobes, big bed, all expensive.

"Bastards." No call for net curtains here—who's going to be looking in and laughing at them?

Three more bedrooms, only one bed unmade.

Although big, none of the bedrooms seems deep enough to go under the whole house. There was a sort of bridge across to the door out front, Martin thinks, remembering skylights below it.

The last windows he looks through feel loose. He examines the window catch. (Each set of windows is a pair, opening outwards.) With a thinner blade he could, Martin thinks, undo this pair's catch. The boys though, he tells himself, being as scruffy as they are, probably aren't being kept in this spick and span house.

He goes on to the double doors. They aren't locked.

Inside is a small, red garden tractor with a rusting trailer attached, and old oil spills on the concrete floor. Around the walls are rakes and bill-hooks, a spade, a pair of oars, a pile of faded blue rope with a red-oxided grappling iron. A yellow canoe is leant against the wall in the far corner, a pile of dry logs beside it. A strimmer looks recently used, as does a black-greased buzz-saw in the trailer, along with new white chips of sawdust.

No-one has been kept in here.

Martin creeps forward to try the door leading into the house. It is locked, tightly fitted, with no play at all in either the handle or the lock.

Tip-toeing out of the store, Martin closes the double doors. Standing there, his face screwed up with indecision, he looks down at the white-silver lake, around at all the trees, and wonders what to do next—what to tell Steve when he gets back.

Thinking this, he starts to retrace his steps, and pauses at the loose window. If the boys are in the house then, having come this far, he has got to find them.

He tries to remember whether he saw any carpentry tools in the store. Can't remember. So he pushes his own screwdriver into the join, past the rubber seal, and tries to position its flat end on the catch. But the thickness of the screwdriver's round haft is pressing the gap back on itself, so that the further in Martin presses the screwdriver, the tighter the join becomes. One good tap, though, he thinks. Martin thumps the blade in and tries again.

He is aware of the noise booming into the house, and pauses to listen for a reaction. He thumps the square end of the blade in again, and wrenches it up. Listens. A sound of metal wheels.

"The gate!" he realises.

Open-mouthed, Martin looks at the white wounds he has inflicted on the dark brown windowframe. He can hear a car bumping slowly up the drive. Reaching down, he grabs up a wormcast, rubs it into the wood, puts his mouth to the crack.

"Simon! Danny!" he shout-whispers, "Hold on. We'll be back for you."

Martin goes leaping across the open ground, down to a path. But, with fear behind him, his legs have lost their spring. He stumbles and trips into the woods. Aware of the noise he must be making, he stops, just as the car engine is turned off. Bent forward, he pulls air into his lungs. A car door slams. Martin creeps off.

Yellow lights come on in the upper windows.

All around the lake Martin can feel the light against the side of his face.

The van now safely parked, Steve walks back up the road and along by the wall. Finding his white-sprayed line, he steps across a ditch and into the woods opposite the wall. Settling to wait, he leans back against a smooth tree trunk and puts his hands in his jacket pockets.

That becomes uncomfortable. He takes his hands out of his pockets, and walks about squirming his shoulders. He finds a moss-softened tree stump, sits on that.

Worry has creased Steve's thoughts all day, and he sinks into worrying thoughts again. He looks around at the thin tree trunks this side of the road, over at the high wall, sighs, and asks himself—what are we doing here? Would Danny have gone off all these days without letting them know? He did once, the time he stole that car. Becoming a gangster would appeal to him. To Steve, though, Dan is still a child, and Steve knows that Danny, like when he crashed the car, will by now be out of his depth. So am I, he thinks.

Should they, like Mary wants, just go to the police now? We'll see what Martin finds out first, Steve decides. And his thoughts circle the worry again.

The car coming up to the gate breaks into the worry. Bending forward from his tree stump seat, Steve can see the side of a dark blue four-wheel drive in front of the gate. The driver is alone, and sits there waiting for the gate to roll back.

Red brake lights go off as the car passes in. Steve listens to the outer gate closing, then the inner gate opening. Picking his damp trousers from his bum and looking to the wall top, Steve goes to the edge of the ditch.

"Come on, come on," he wills Martin to hear. And he decides that he definitely doesn't want to be here. He can see no end of trouble coming from this. The inner gate starts to close.

"Come on, come on."

Should he fetch the van before Martin gets to the wall? Get the ladder and board set up and ready? But what if someone else comes along to the gate and sees the van parked there? How'll he explain the ladder? What if Sweets find out he's using the van out of work? There'll be hell to pay. And Steve likes his job. Gets him out and about.

"Come on."

He hears Martin's voice.

"Yeah?"

"The van!" Martin gasps from somewhere in the tree. "Get the fuckin' van. Hurry!"

Martin watches fat, little Steve start to run, flat-footed, along the road—only to give that up and continue in a quick, waddling walk, his bald head jerking side to side.

"Run you fat bastard," Martin says quietly. "Run."

He can feel the trembling from his exhausted arms and legs radiating out through the tree, and imagines a pair of binoculars coming to rest on the treetop's quivering leaves, dogs being loosened, guards sent off to investigate ...

Its headlights off, the van comes looming white through the dusk, and parks directly beneath the branch. At least he's got that right, Martin thinks. As soon as Steve goes round the back, Martin starts edging out along the branch. He winces as the van's back roller squeaks up.

With the branch bending under him, Martin waits until Steve comes up the ladder with the board.

"Can't you put some fuckin' grease on that fuckin' door?"

"It's where the slats go in the grooves."

"So grease the fuckers."

Martin, slipping, lets himself drop onto the board.

"Can't use grease," Steve says, "Gets on the furniture."

"Fuck the furniture." Martin hands the screwdriver to Steve. The yellow plastic is hot from Martin's hand.

Steve is still stood on top of the ladder, looking over the roof for damage. He is in Martin's way.

"Come on!"

Steve moves. As soon as he can, Martin gets on the ladder, brings down the board with him, and slides it in the back of the van. Steve lets the ladder down.

"Find them?" he asks Martin.

"Not today. Convinced they're there though—locked inside the house."

"Yeah?"

"Come on," Martin says, standing on the van's tail to pull down the door. "Let's get outa here."

In the overgrown gateway, where the van was parked, a hen blackbird comes running out of the brambles. She pecks among the wheel-torn divots.

# 13

Since you weren't there, sister, my life, my half life, seems to have been about seeking wholeness, oneness.

I am a half. A loose half.

Even as a teenager my hunger for another was such that I attached myself to girls with such jealous passion that I must have terrified the life out of them. And this before, technically, I lost my virginity.

(How does one put a precise date to when one has lost one's virginity? I don't want to seem coy about it, but virginity is not lost of a moment. Rather it is an erosion of innocence, snippet upon snippet—the knowledge having arrived long before theory becomes fact—that one act lost in a heap of knowing. I can only date my being a virgin by deciding on a date when I'm sure I didn't know. And I cannot date such an innocence.)

The whole of my life I've been a half, seeking to make myself whole in the flesh of another. I crept, skinny and naked, into my nannies' beds. Most made me get out. Two of them giggled and let me stay, and made me promise not to tell. Nannies get lonely.

Adolescence, sex, gave that urge cause. But no-one— no-one I knew then—could figure out how those very ordinary looking girls could arouse such passions. Such impossible passions.

Every generation, sister, has to think it invented sex. (There are many such natural blindnesses necessary to the process of life.) Consequently, most children deny the sex life of their parents—the very sex life that created them. But our parents' sex life was on film for all the world to see. Both of them with various other actors. I therefore had more to deny, more to prove, more to invent.

My adolescence was a very confusing time for all concerned.

Young people—in the process of life—go seeking someone, something, worthy of their love. Who, what, they choose is their estimation of themselves. I, though, had to own whomever it was I chose. I had to have their flesh constantly next to mine, striving to merge with their flesh, to be in each minute of their time. To be another. To be whole.

They were young like me, and such overwhelming needs were too much for them. Between those girls and I— there were many tears and sobbings and cryings out in the night.

I know now, perhaps knew then, that I wanted them to be you. I tried to turn them into you, into what I imagined you'd be. Possession had to be total—my love, my creation. "I need to breathe," one said. She was actually gasping. "I need to breathe."

I know now that I was forcing them into scripts of my choosing. People, I know now, aren't capable of that. You're irreplaceable, sister.

At the same time, mine was the idealistic, the unsatisfiable love, of any young man who places himself in an heroic role—only to have base and carnal woman, time and again, thwart that misconceived notion of himself.

Oh, the folly of spent passions.

I laid myself open to some very ordinary girls. I begged. I cried. I pleaded. I promised eternal love—

anything, but don't leave me. Don't leave me. None of those very ordinary, unambitious girls wanted me. Maybe if I'd been a little more reticent, a little safer, they'd have snapped up such a sure prospect of a husband.

Maybe they were right, having sensed that I wasn't such a sure prospect. Because, at the same time as making those emotional deals—you-love-me-and-I'll-love you—I resented them making me the least part of their lives. I refused to let any of them think that I was imbued with the least of their values. I'd just escaped, was still escaping, our parents, and so was not prepared to let myself become another's property.

The next lot of women who came into my life were very sure of their good looks, and had the confidence both to take me on and to dump me. Because, by this time, my criminal career made me dangerous to know. And danger is, of course, attractive to women.

Most young women, sister, are unadmittedly bisexual. From their girlfriends they draw sensual comfort—brush one another's hair, compare skin types, try on each other's clothes, share scents. In men, orgasm is the prime objective, in fact it's the biological purpose of their existence; all other pleasures, therefore, all sensual comforts, are merely accomplices to ejaculation. Women, however, gain equal pleasure from other bodily functions. Consummation, thus, is not always devoutly desired. Ergo, the incompatibility of the sexes.

Men also look to women to provide comfort. Women, receiving sufficient comfort from their friends, look to men for excitement. While women continue to be attracted to men who excite, to men who emanate a sense of menace, those same men will continue to beat them. And, knowing that, some women will reject all men in advance—or as soon as she feels herself attracted to a man.

There is, however, only so much rejection a body can take. Despising them for being attracted to a thug like me, I loved them for their scented transparency, but hated myself for loving them. I was betrayed by them too, and caught them out in silly infidelities. Only to have them turn on me a blaze of guilty defiance.

By which time, cynical of all women, I simply made use of them. With many I saw myself, indifferent to them, as only a proficient sexual technician, without passion. I can recall, even now, heroic feats of pork swordsmanship. And many, who then came to me, wanted to be used this way. Sex was like an enactment of hatred, a self-fulfilling disgust of both of us for ourselves.

By my early twenties I was sick of such women. All were flawed like me. These two negatives multiplied our hatred, and I could see in it a destructive cycle. And, by then, I was tired of living only destruction.

I had escaped our parents, had created my own past, and had my own base measures. Now I wanted to create, to make, so I looked for a wife.

I wasn't looking for love. Love requires honesty, and I couldn't be honest—it would be far too dangerous for whomever I was honest with. (If it was thought that my beloved knew what I knew, they could be made to tell.) I had to choose carefully the woman who could be my wife. It was thus a calculated move.

Also, by this time, many of my colleagues were married. I was becoming uncomfortable at social gatherings. Viewed by the married, the single are seen to be dangerous, incomplete, unsettled and unsettling people. Being single, they are assumed to be, always, on the lookout for another life to slot into. Once slotted, once 'complete', they can look out from their partnership with equanimity, and can be relied upon not to upset other pairings. The single, like a carriage without a train, must be always looking for a coupling to get themselves back on track. I was seen as a threat to every marriage.

So I took myself on an ordinary holiday, away from gangsters, and away from women who were attracted to gangsters. And in that seaside resort I coolly appraised each girl I met, even the waitresses and shop assistants who served me.

In that first week, Fay was one of three I watched. One of the others laughed too loudly, and came to look like a pleasure-seeker. The other was too concerned about money. But Fay smiled slowly, talked softly, and was religious. A religious type seemed right. They don't question.

I wooed her, won her for the holiday romance, and travelled up to see her when she returned home.

Love, sister, is a social process. An essential part of that process is each proponent having to win the love of the other—for only by having won it, will they value it. Fay wrote me affectionate but non-committal letters. I phoned.

These weekend visits I kept up for about three months. Then we took a holiday together. Marriage plans came about almost as a natural occurrence.

Although our courtship was artificial, and calculated in almost every detail, I was happy as I'd never been happy before. And my calculated approach didn't preclude spontaneity. The planning was in arranging the time and place for the marriage. Of the first months of the marriage itself, all I can remember is laughter.

I'm not saying that Fay replaced you, sister, but in those first years of marriage, you receded.

Of course Fay gradually found out the true nature of

my business activities. (Fay was actually more put out that
I'd kept the true identity of our parents from her. Until she
got to know them that is. Then she became—outwardly—
more angry at their actorish self-obsession than I'd ever
been. Fay's idea of what grandparents should be like did not
coincide with their idea of the role. And a 'role' is exactly
how they saw it.)

Fay measured my treatment of her against that of a
couple of previous boyfriends who'd casually made use of
her. Such was Fay's character, that already in her short life
she'd twice been owned by others' expectations. And twice
she'd been reluctant to voice her disavowal, to say 'no, I
don't want that'—in order not to hurt or offend. So two
men had walked over this soft human being on their way to
the grave.

Fay also saw the house I provided and how I was
determined that my other life shouldn't touch her or the
children. She reconciled herself to ignoring the stories of
my other life.

That other life killed her. Was she foolish?

I miss her. I miss having her to tell the little things to.
I hate being single. I hate coming back home and seeing
everything just as I left it.

Almost. Almost as I left it.

I was coming back from my morning walk in the
garden just now. I've got different circuits I do. This one
brings me up past the round stair window. (Built on a slope,
the stairs follow the slope up inside the house.) Under the
window were skid marks. And around one of the big
downstairs windows the wood had been splintered by a
knife or a jemmy.

The house windows are all double-glazed and locked.
So unless they have specialised burglar's tools, or the whole

window is taken out, there's no way anyone can get into the house. What worries me most is that they've got into the garden. I made two quick circuits of the walls and I still can't figure out where. It can't be where the last lot of intruders got over. I lopped off the two overlapping branches, and I went right round the outside checking for others. Then how? Where?

A puzzle. A worry.

# 14

Sister Clare,

I want to justify, through you, my relationship with my children. My non-relationship with my children. With my two surviving children.

Your niece and nephew, Marilyn and Oliver, are not twins. Marilyn is older by fifteen months.

I wasn't sure, all four times that Fay was pregnant, whether I wanted twins or not. I still don't know if I was disappointed or relieved by all those single births. I know for certain that, whether or not it might have been good for me, it wouldn't have been good for the children. If both twins had lived beyond birth I'd have been too watchful, too curious, waiting to see what it would have been like for you and me.

And, of course, it wouldn't have been anything like that. I wouldn't have been our father.

Children are consequences. They are a culmination— at any one time—of a host of tiny acts. Children also exist, ultimately, beyond their parents' control. And the parents know this: offspring will one day spring off. To the parents, children are, therefore, not so emotionally charged—not so emotionally loaded as the parents are to the children. The parents are the past, and the past cannot be altered, cannot even be wholly remembered. The past is.

Mal and Ollie are now at that age when they—Mal and Ollie anyway—want to find fault with their parents.

And Fay and I were a couple of easy targets. Fay was so
slapdash careless that she went and got herself killed. And I
am the one who brought about, indirectly, her death. Easy,
therefore, to find fault with the two of us.

Of course, Mal and Ollie, new to being parents, are
going to be perfect parents. As were Fay and I.

It goes down the generations this, no matter how
earnestly you try to stop it. Fay and I didn't want our
children to be contaminated by our parents; and we fell out
with hers as well. Then we swore it wouldn't happen with
our own grandchildren. But neither Mal nor Ollie now
bring their children to see me, their grandfather. And both,
saying it's for the safety of their children, have forbidden me
to come to their houses.

I send cards and money. We sometimes talk on the
phone. Or rather they shout at me on the phone. "Don't
you care?! I didn't see you crying! Not once! Too used to
death you are!"

They're probably right. Like I said before, the dead
are dead, they simply stopped there. The living go on, with
the ordinary things that the living do.

Yes, sister, they still take my money, my tainted money.
Sometimes I think I'd have more respect for them, more
love even, if they threw the money back in my face. But of
course they don't.

Fay's parents couldn't be bought. They voiced their
disapproval of me, of what the papers said about me. They
didn't visit. And Fay disapproved of our shallow parents, and
didn't encourage them to visit. At least I'm punctilious in
remembering birthdays.

I do love Mal and Ollie, both of them. And my love
isn't conditional. It doesn't depend on how pretty or clever
they are. But neither is it active. I don't know how to bridge

this gap. If it is bridgeable.

It was simple when they were young. This was a place of laughter. The children out in the woods all day, in orange canoes on the lake. Fay encouraged all their friends back to play. It was all such good fun.

The young are immortal, they live in a young-time eternity. Newly arrived to the light—this is, has been, will always be. Fay and I, as their young parents, shared in that enchanted time.

I played the role of doting father, did all that I felt was expected of me. I went and saw their teachers, watched the school plays. (Mal and Ollie weren't encouraged: I didn't want any more actors in the family.) And those times Fay couldn't make it, I went along to the doctor and dentist with them. I was, I am, a good father.

Of course, as they got older, my profession caused them problems. Most children are naturally idealistic. They see rights and wrongs in simple terms. The young also have a yearning for spontaneity, for—in themselves—moments of pure passion, uncorrupted by planning, by ulterior motives. It was hard, therefore, to reconcile themselves to a cold and calculating gangster father.

At home, however, I refused to talk about the ins and outs of my chosen profession, just used to say, "That's business" and leave it at that. They—Mal mostly—would get a bit hot under the collar, throw newspaper allegations at me; and I'd shrug. "My business." I'd say. Got to be a family joke come the end.

Try as we might to be good parents, none of us can know in what way we are flawed, nor how those flaws are going to manifest themselves. We, as parents, avoid the obvious—to us—pitfalls. But time moves on, and the older we get, the more time we spend looking back, not forward.

The future, the children's future, doesn't matter as much to us, as they get older, as it does to them.

I'm not saying that I didn't make mistakes. When Mal was thirteen—with her long legs and small, hard breasts—one of my runners looked her over with a rapist's contempt. We were all at a friend's house. It was their toddler's birthday party, and Mal was playing at being aunty—helping with games, wiping mouths, etc. (Mal's good with animals too. She's had horses, rabbits, cats, dogs. Parakeets once. This place was so quiet when she left.)

I employed—made use of—this particular runner because he was ruthless. He was also stupid—especially to have let me see him looking at my daughter like that. Stupidity which got him killed.

It wasn't until a couple of years later that Mal found out. I think she'd been flirting with another of my staff and he'd said something like, "You've got to be joking. After what your Dad did to ..." At least that's what I guess was said, because Mal made sure that I never got enough of the story to identify anyone.

Which was one of the main reasons I got rid of the staff. Having them around was always a hindrance to family life. Their trailing around after me also advertised that I thought myself to be worth guarding.

Most of the guards went when we first moved here within the wall. Then, when my capital became entirely respectable, I dispensed with them altogether. (Even after Fay's death: they couldn't have stopped that.)

I made mistakes with Ollie too. Different mistakes, mind.

Ollie was like Fay.

There are traits in our sexual partners that we can despise, but we don't dare mention them, in case our feelings become clear and we drive our loved ones away. But those same traits, inherited by and evident in our children, we carp on and criticise with all the unspent force of redirected repression. And we say that we're doing it in the name of love.

Isn't hindsight a wonderful thing? Nullifies crimes. Poor Ollie.

I used to loath Fay's head-dropping acquiescence. Of course I had no right to voice my irritation at it, since her submissiveness had been the principle character trait that had attracted me to her. Whenever poor Oliver, however, dropped his head, I'd be barking at him to "Hold your head up boy! Speak clearly! Don't slink away from me mumbling. Stay and argue!" And I'd be in a real passion over it.

All quite ridiculous now, of course. Poor Ollie. The childhoods we inflict on our children. Mistakes that get twisted about and repeated down the generations, like an erosive drip wearing us all away.

Had Fay not been killed, I reckon, given time, that both Ollie and Mal would have reconciled themselves to my business, which anyway is now wholly legal. Both of them would have brought their partners home to meet us.

Ollie's wife was round-eyed with fear the first time she visited. The second time she flirted—not on the promise of anything sexual, but like lots of young women do with older men they like. While Mal's husband tried to be matey. Even Fay raised an eyebrow. I was polite. Fay fussed and worried what they'd think of us.

I think I must have already been an Acceptor. I knew then that our grown children do not have to explain themselves to us. Their own children will want explanations from them in turn. And there'll be no explanations. Only disconnected histories.

That it's been difficult for Mal and Ollie, I can't deny.
They didn't understand Fay nor I, nor our relationship. To
be frank, I'm not sure that I truly understand it.

I think, in the beginning, Fay and I made a deal—each
our own version—and stuck to it. I don't think we examined
the ins and outs of our relationship much. We were both
busy—she was bringing up Mal and Ollie, and I had my
work. We got on with what we had to do, and the years
passed. Most of what we talked about together, I suppose,
was what was best for the children, and how not to spoil
them.

Without realising it, I think, Fay and I got used to one
another. Later, with Mal and Ollie not needing her so
much, and with my work settled into a pattern, she looked
at me and I looked at her, and we both realised that we were
fond of one another. You could almost say that Baby Bonny
and little Darren were our love-children.

Or you could say that Fay, being given less and less to
do by Mal and Ollie, looked to recreate the role in which
she'd been happiest, by becoming pregnant again. I don't
honestly think so: we'd both changed so much. No, our
relationship was as complex as any other. We'd moved on.

The simplest fact of life is that we are all, we human
beings, here to produce more of us. Which is why love and
sex are so important to us, why they so endlessly fascinate. It
makes us endless.

For this second breeding, I was certainly in love with
Fay as I have never loved anyone before. Not even you,
sister. Because this was a tangible love. When Fay was
pregnant, for instance, and she got those inward-looking
eyes of pregnant women—such clear whites, the irises a
varnished brown, the black pupils absorbing the world
which was becoming her baby—I'd look up to find her

regarding me with a loving candour, and I'd feel myself fill with tenderness for her.

Mal and Ollie are now applying other rules to our 'relationship'. Mal and Ollie each their own set of rules. The real relationship that Fay and I had though, with all its conventional failings—we didn't talk, that is off-load to one another—that flawed relationship, whether they like it or not, is what produced the pair of them. They can't, however, seem to accept that. Both of them want Fay and I to have been other than how we really were, to have been perfect in some way known only to them.

Mal owns too that sentimental selfishness common to all animal lovers: a kind of egotism, simply projecting one's self onto the animal loved. It's a narrowminded love, a love that feeds one kind of captive animal to another kind of captive animal. How can one distinguish which is worthy of love—the eater or the eaten? And she calls me callous.

For all our failings, Fay and I were real. And I got Fay, baby Bonny and little Darren killed. We three, the survivors, we're all of us going to have to learn to live with that.

# 15

Mary is uncomfortable in this over-furnished house of knick-knacks. Even the doorhandles are wooden—they have been lathe-turned, and then carved into acorn or fir-cone shapes. (Tina once said that the acorn handles looked like a young girl's tit: Martin, not wanting to be seen as a lecher, has been looking for an excuse to change them ever since.)

Mary keeps signalling for Steve to sit down beside her.

She still feels sticky from the wet outside. Her and Steve's anoraks were left to drip in the hallway. Her hair is flattened, and her tights are clinging to her knees. She wants Steve to sit next to her, but Steve seems to want to stand and talk man-to-man with Martin.

"What's going on now?" she says.

"Short answer is, Mary," Martin says all deep and solemn, moving to stand with his legs apart, "we don't know."

"We should go to the police," Mary gathers herself on the sofa, "before it's too late."

They have already wasted a whole day. Nothing was decided last night when the men got back—just talk, just thinking what might have happened, or might not. Nothing definite was known. And now, after a day of all of them being at work and doing nothing, there was more talk.

"We should go to the police now," Mary offered again.

Steve has moved to stand beside her, puts his hand on her shoulder, and says, "Martin still thinks they might be locked in there. If we get the police involved, then there's no telling what might happen. He might just get rid of them, so there's no evidence."

"You said yesterday they were probably working for him. I'm going to the police."

But she doesn't stand up.

The start of all this was Mary telling her worries to a kind old woman at work—one of the physically ill. Mary hadn't known how worried she was until she'd told her.

"You must be worried sick," the old woman had said. She didn't know her Dan though, Mary thought. But the more Mary dwelled on the old woman saying how worried she must be, the more worried she actually got, until at last she had a go at Steve. And now—since he and Martin have been going up there—she can tell no-one at all what's going on. So the worry just goes round and round inside her head and her stomach. Now it seems to be holding her down.

Steve and Tina are looking to Martin. Martin, not knowing what to say to Mary, looks over to Nathan, who is standing with his back to them all. He is looking out at the silver, dripping rain.

"They're still alive," Martin declares. "I know it. So what you crying for?" he asks Nathan.

"They're going to say ..." Nathan gulps back his tears. "They're going to say ..."

"Say what?" Martin takes a step towards him. Tina reaches out her hand to Martin's arm.

"What you trying to say, Nate?" Martin asks him, leaning forward.

"They're going to say it was my fault they was caught."

"No, they're not." Straightening, Martin turns from him. "They'll be only too pleased to have been found."

All listen to Nathan sniff.

"They been gone too long," Mary says. "We should be telling the police."

"Look ..." Martin begins. This twitching, dithering red-eyed woman makes him want to shout. "I said it might be the worse thing we do. You want us to get 'em killed?"

Martin knows how to win arguments, how to battle his protagonists into silence—but not how to persuade the reluctant to accept his point of view.

"I want my boy found," Mary says, straightening up out of her snivelling. "And I don't see you finding him. All I see is you and him playing detectives."

"No, we're not ..." Steve whines in protest, patting her shoulder.

Martin grunts.

Tina looks down on Mary, crouching back inside her worry, and tells herself that she knows how Mary must be feeling. Tina herself is still numb. Something has happened to her son. Until she finds out what it is, she, as usual, will not let herself feel. In the meantime, she has to keep the peace.

"You still reckon they're in the house?" she says to Martin.

Stiff and sore from the running and climbing, Martin felt that he'd spent half the night finding a comfortable position and half the night telling her this bare fact.

"At the back," he explains again, exasperated. "You can't see 'em."

"How do you know they're in there then?"

"I know." Martin rocks his anger inside himself. "I know."

He doesn't know. He wants them to be there and he wants to be the one who rescues them. And he doesn't want

Dan's silly weeping mother to stop him.

"Tell you what," Tina says, "you and Steve go back up there, and have one more go at getting 'em out. If you can't, then me and Mary'll go to the police. OK?"

Martin frowns, angry at having been questioned, at his word having been doubted openly. But Martin knows when to stop pushing his wife—Tina's eyes go narrow and a stubbornness, directed at him, enters her every movement.

"How can you say that before we even find out what's there?" It's a lawyer's question.

"I don't care," Tina says. "You got one more chance to find out. Alright, Mary? We go to the police tomorrow."

"We can't go up there tonight," Martin says, raising his large, work-yellowed palms. "He'll be home. We can't get into his house while he's at home."

"I'm going to the police tomorrow." Mary has stiffened into resolution.

"Look." Martin stoops to her, doesn't know how to convince her, but knows that swearing at her won't help. "Look—if we can get this sorted out ourselves, it just becomes a good story we can tell sometime. With the police involved ... well, that makes us the centre of attention here."

Mary doesn't know what he's talking about.

"Tomorrow afternoon," Steve tells her. "Go to the police tomorrow afternoon. Saturday. After we've checked it out one more time."

Mary sees him glance to Martin for approval.

"OK?" Tina asks her.

Mary nods.

# 16

Steve can taste the tiredness at the back of his lips. He wants to sink this day into the pillow; but, cuddling up behind Mary, he feels the warm comfortable division of her buttocks.

Smiling his thought into the dark, he slides his hand up to her tit.

"How could you?" she whispers, throwing his arm off. "Time like this?" She bounces away from him.

"Sorry." Steve turns his back to her, but doesn't—his eyes open to the dark—see why they shouldn't. At a time like this.

# 17

Sister, tell me—do I need to do anything about these people?

There were more marks this morning. First thing I saw—opened my bedroom curtains and there it was—a handprint on the outside of the glass. One greased palm-print among the night's condensation. They're not afraid to be known. I'd say they mean to frighten me. But how are they getting into the garden? Flying?

I am now afraid for my safety, sister.

But should I be? Do I matter? Does it matter now what happens to me?

Or is that the depression of my unexpressed grief talking? Or age? The depression of age?

Because I am old and shrivelling, sister. I am disappearing inside my increasing body hair. And never, even at my gloomiest, did I imagine that getting old would be a matter of so many aches and inconvenient twinges.

To be this old is a surprise. I look at the old man in the mirror and I see an imposter.

To be perceived by others as this old is a surprise too. In here, with you, I'm still young and unfinished. I'm still finding out, barely begun.

This is nothing new, sister. I have, as you know, watched myself grow old, with amazement that it should be happening to me—to me who had thought a moment was a lifetime and have lived so many moments. But—this I know, knew—we are never wholly in control—not of ourselves, nor of our bodies.

First, when young, our bodies surprise us with their rapid growth—we have to grow inside them. (You did not, did not, sister. Why not?) Then they surprise us by being so sturdy—after all the abuse we heap upon them. Then their frailty, their fragility, their mortality also makes us look anew at them—a germ, a virus, or a toothache can undo us.

Lastly, with age, our shape changes again. We still feel big, but our bodies shrink and our skin shrivels. The consequence is that, throughout our lives, we are never physically wholly at one with ourselves. And mentally ... mentally we simply can't remember—not everything. Who can recall the whole of their formative childhood?

All that we have are partial memories. And we can't even trust them. Yet memories are the fabric of our identities.

People are in awe of the accumulation of years, yet a single moment is more likely to change a life. I have been a lover, a man of passion, and a man hard in muscle, feeling and judgement. Not this podgy, dithering old geezer, quick to fears and sentimental tears—frightened by a single palm-print.

A single palm-print, sister, a single palm-print. I am an old man. To the young I am already passed, complete, done. The surprise there, sister, is to discover in one's self a piece of living history, already a legend.

I first realised I was old, sister, when people younger than me declared a nostalgia for what I still think of as now.

But I accept my age, sister. I try to accept my age. Age is a part of change. And change is what the people I listen to won't accept. They want to freeze time—at some point in the past—to be themselves, one's self, one time, to all own the illusion that one day the past will return to them in perfect health. But it cannot be.

I sit and I listen to the pursuit of such impossible dreams. They forecast certainty of disappointment. But those I listen to now are in despair—they are already disappointed people. Solely because, when young, they didn't actively seek experience. No, they tried to avoid it. Now old, and intimates of tragedy and pain, they have no experience to fall back on. I look across at them with their lives of emotionless mediocrity, their lives that have never known yearning, that have never been foolish. What a very respectable person, I sit there and think: what a waste of a life.

Then there are those for whom a single, strong passion has shaped their life—a loved person, or an all-encompassing past-time—and then, the thing having finished, left them passionless. They are left a feeble and agitated observer of their own degeneration.

I sit there and I listen to these tales of woe, and I know that I'm never going to be young again. I do though, sister, accept my age. I will not become one of those old men who idealise their imperfect past—either its body shape or its passing friendships—and then try impossibly to get back to it. Each age has its priorities. Mine now is to be left here in peace with my garden.

Every time I think that, I see the palm-print on my bedroom window.

I want rid of these new intruders, whoever they are. Simply get rid of them. Not vengeance. The only cruelty I crave now is the sadistic pleasure to be had from dead-heading roses. And that is a constructive cruelty, for it produces more flowers.

Such are an old man's pleasures. Because at this age,

my age, there is no purpose, no real purpose to my life. I'm
not now going to meet and marry, fall in love. This sagging
sack of bones is going to be no-one's new object of desire.
Nor do I want it to be. Fay and I grew together—grew stout
together like a pair of trees, and got wrinkled together. I
don't now desire another wrinkled woman. (Although, with
a woman my own age, we could perhaps share the same
landmarks, know where we are.)

No, I don't want a woman of any age, even if well-
preserved. Especially if well-preserved. They are the blank-
faced women, sister. These are the women who have learnt
to put on the make-up, the masks of the good-looking.
About them, though, about them all, is a look of incipient
despair. The question their eyes ask, as they enter every
room new to them—is this all there is?

I sit there and I listen to them without expression. And
I know too that I am a victim of similar conditioning. Male,
I own pre-programmed responses to signals—particularly
those given off by female display. I feel my eyes being
drawn, despite myself, to bare female arms, exposed thighs,
breasts, etc. This basic conditioning is difficult to resist.

It is far easier these days, however, not to act on it.
The idea of a feeble old man screwing a sturdy young
woman—it's a genetic obscenity. There's the thought too,
the self-image, of an old man's lust—a lust often incapable
of his desires. And yet, yet the old man's desires are
insatiable and, against his will, he becomes obsessed with
young flesh, with the might-have-beens of his own life.

A bullish, powerful old man need not, I suppose, be
quite so obscene. He's the leader of the herd, of the pack,
passing on his powerful genes. And there are plenty of
young women around, sister, who will let me put my sex
into them. I am rich and, no matter how I came by my

riches, wealth equals power. All of which is not to say that these young women can be bought cheaply, rather that—having been bought—they will then invest me with other physical attractions.

There is also a yearning, sister, that comes with age: a wanting to touch and to hold again sweet, firm flesh and, in touching, to be young yourself again. This yearning can easily be mistaken, in one's self, for lechery. It is not lechery. It is a yearning rather for how things were or might have been, and a sadness comes because it can never be again, because we are wrinkled and unattractive to ourselves.

We will never be young again. No girl is ever again going to take real pleasure in smoothing her hands over my body. She might, because of who I am, let me smooth my old hands over her body. To pursue half a dream, though, is doubly unsatisfactory.

If she were to look beyond the payment, then with long familiarity, such a young woman might, yes might, come to love me. But it would not be a physical love. It would be, at best, an affection for me. And anything less than total love, love despite herself, would not be enough.

So I prefer to look, just look, at such young women—all fire and thighs—and I dream of what kind of man they might have made of me when I was young.

Powerful I may be; but I'm no leader of the pack, about to perpetuate forcefully his genes. All that I want, sister, is to be left alone here with you.

Sister, what would you have looked like if you were here and alive now? Would your hair have been thick and white like mine? Wavy? Long? White and folded like a meringue?

You, like me, would not have tried to be artificially young. We know that our time is past. We know that our own generation must always be like giants, striding out onto our stage—with all those who went before, and all those who will come after, mere bit players. We are the giants. Stories will be told about us, by us.

Now we are old, sister. We are no more the history-makers. Here I am in this aged body with you, sister, and a store of imperfect memories. And this is nothing new for us. It is a collection, an accumulation, of those moments that placed us in the background. It happens to every one of us. When you realise that no-one wants you for their future, that no-one new wants to take you into their future. That, having done all that you're ever going to do, you don't figure, can't figure, in the future of anyone unmet.

By the time anyone reaches forty, they've been around so long, have survived so much, they can start to suffer the delusion that they're permanent. Come fifty-seven, and no-one wants to make me a part of their life. Already I am all past and no future. And the new cannot belong to my past.

I sit down in my office, sister, and I listen to people who are lost in time, and I drift off.

Science, sister, will make us re-define humanity. A human being can no longer be his or her function—parent, job, whatever. Now automation takes away jobs. Longevity negates the species function of parenthood. Now we are that and more. That which we do, that which we make, that place where we are, are part of us, but no longer the whole. How can all this spare capacity of being human fit together? Are we mere producers and consumers? Or are we to see ourselves now as part of the greater humanity? Where is this greater humanity bound?

All I am now is my own past.

All I am now is in the way. And someone is trying to remove me.

The young are greedy. They want what I have got.
No, not greedy. They just want more.

The young detest compromise. The middle-aged
delight in it and call it realism. I remember when I was
young—wanting to be, without reservation, immersed in
the moment. To be wholly in that moment: completely
there, and not watching myself from any remove.

I felt I was always watching. Or you were.

Well, no, not always.

In times of little change, we can build illusions about
ourselves, and create selves that are illusions. When changes
come quickly, one after the other, we become reactive
beings, made by the moment. Although I may have been the
one, often, to have instigated a series of rapid reactions, they
were not, ultimately, in my control. I was made by those
moments.

Sometimes, sister, I think I've done too good a job of
staying alive, that I was never meant to get this old—old
enough to learn doubt—doubt of all I've ever been told,
doubt of myself, doubt of my own powers, desires, conceits.

I cannot now rely on the past as deterrent. What's
gone has no power to change. Now is all there is.

I wonder if these intruders even know who I am. Who
I was. I am as old, now, as those I once looked upon with
awe. The ones I fought, who feared me, were soldiers my
own age—all old now, or dead.

All that is mine now is this garden, and contempt from
Mal and Ollie.

As a first-time father, I existed on the periphery of my
children's lives. Occasionally I might have come to figure
centrally in their minds, but only as a focus of resentment,
of hatred. In actuality, my contact is minimal. I am
occasional. And this is not peculiar to me. I see other

parents sidelined in their children's lives. We are done, over, of the past, finished.

My infamy is not the issue here. Like the backstage gossip about our parents, it was distasteful to me, that was all. As is my gangster-rumoured past. Because, although children may be curious—occasionally—about the scandalous past of their parents, they don't truly care. It doesn't matter to their lives. Mal and Ollie have their own pasts to create, as I did.

After all that, what I want from life now, sister, is to be again attuned to the moment, instead of having this distance from it. I want those days again when I awoke feeling that I had the bite on life. Instead of days which are only periods of wakefulness.

Lately of fear.

Or is this just me getting older? All I want now is peace and comfort. And they won't leave me alone.

Is it solely the young? I am not, I am sure, one of those old men who, envious of them, hates the young, and is contemptuous of them and all that they do. To me the young are simply new. I am simply old.

# 18

Saturday morning, and there are still showers. A squall rocks the empty van as they rise up beyond Estley. Before they reach the top of the hill, they have come out the other side of the squall.

This time Steve doesn't take the fork, but drives on to the other junction to bring him back past the gate. He drives slowly. They see nothing.

Martin tells him to stop a bit further on, where the curve of the wall will take the van out of sight of the gate. Steve comes to a halt at a dry, grey spot under a large tree.

Martin, practised now, sends the back squeaking up just far enough for Steve to reach in and start pulling out the ladder. Martin takes it from him, places it against the back of the van and starts climbing. Steve has meanwhile slid out the board and steps up the ladder behind Martin's heels. Martin takes the board from him, lays it on the roof, clambers around onto it, grabs a branch, pulls it down hand over hand, swings himself up, and starts crawling along it over the top of the wall.

Steve pulls the board towards himself, carries it down the ladder and slides it back into the van. The shortened ladder follows it. He pulls the shutter down and trots to the front, takes out his aerosol of white paint and sprays a line on the dry part of the road.

Martin, having reached the ground, scrapes his heel-line through the copper-wet leaf litter by the tree. He waits to hear the van leave.

This day, the stillness of the woods is punctuated by drips and dribbles from leaf to leaf.

When the van engine starts, Martin sets off along the same paths as before.

This day he doesn't run: after all the unaccustomed exercise, Martin's calf and shin muscles were yesterday tender even to the touch. In places, his feet squelch.

Away across the glinting indigo lake, another squall is building, violet-grey in the sky. In the upstairs windows of the house are yellow lights. From here Martin can't see the downstairs.

The storm reaches Martin when he is almost at the lake's end. He shelters in the lee of an old oak's gargoyled trunk, watches the wind tear wet, flapping leaves and small twigs from branch ends, listens to the rain hissing into the disordered canopy, and sees it striking like needles into the open glade.

Martin waits until he is sure that the squall has passed and the wind has eased. He creeps on.

His next glimpse of the house shows that all its lights are out.


Steve brought his grubby, orange anorak from the van back up the road with him this morning. He thought he could use it to sit on even if it doesn't rain. It does rain.

Finding shelter among the thin trees opposite this part of the wall is difficult. The only trees worth sheltering under are further along, towards the gate. And the first of them has a soggy marsh on its sheltered side.

Heading towards the next big tree, Steve sees a car's yellow lights shining off the wet metal of the opening gate. Caught in the open, Steve moves so that the driver's line of sight places him behind the tree. Peeping around it, he sees that it's the same car as before, with again only the driver inside.

When the red lights have disappeared, Steve runs up to the tree trunk, and leans panting with his back to it. His breath blows raindrops off his nose. He hates being here, being frightened. He wants this to be over, to be done with. Now, at least, with the man gone out, if the two boys are in the house, Martin should be able to find them.

Feet in the wet, Steve waits. Waiting, he wonders how he got to be here in these woods on a wet day, wonders how he got to be a father at all. He doesn't feel like a father. He doesn't, like Mary, spend hours worrying about Julie and Dan. Mostly Steve goes from day to day doing what's next to be done. Only sometimes, thinking that he's not—judging by the results—doing it right, does he think about what he should be doing as a father.

His own father buggered off before he can remember. As did his sisters' fathers. He has five sisters. They all call him Fat Boy. Steve's mother spoilt him. His sisters despised him.

Steve met Mary when she came with her friend to visit his friend. The four of them went around in Steve's mini. (His mother's new bloke had helped pay for it.)

The other two, Steve and Mary's friends, broke up. Steve and Mary kept going, until Steve moved in with Mary and her mother in Hambrook. When Mary fell pregnant with Julie they got their own house in Hambrook.

At first Steve went home once a month to visit his own mother. But, whichever of his sisters happened to be there, she criticised him for not visiting more often. Eventually he gave up going. None of his family have visited him.

Steve has tried to treat his children differently. He still

doesn't know, though, what he's doing that's so wrong.

Even here, in the wet, with time to spare, he can't figure it out.

Trousers wet and tight to his knees, Martin crouches beside the floor-length bedroom window. He unzips a rag roll from his jacket pocket. From out of the rag—each wrapped separately so they wouldn't rattle—Martin lays out the tools he brought with him. On the flattened rag, like on a surgeon's tray, are a thin-bladed knife, a pair of pliers, two chisels, three wooden wedges, a nail punch and a small tack hammer. He has thought all night of this moment.

First he slips the pliable knife through the gap between the dark polythene seals and presses up the drop latch. Pulling the window frame towards him, he then forces a wedge up under the knife. Next he takes a strip of tin and slides it, bent in around the frame, to try to catch one of the bottom door bolts. He feels it slip by. He tries again, feels it catch, slip by.

Taking out the piece of tin he curves it some more, feeds it through again. And again he feels it catch, slip by.

Leaving that he takes the other piece of tin—both cut last night and experimented with at home—and, standing up, he tries the top bolt. This catches straightaway and the first bolt drops.

The upper part of the window frame can now be pulled towards him. Wedge and knife drop with a tinkle out of the middle. He reaches his fingers around and pulls down the other bolt.

Both windows being long, there's enough bend in them to allow him to put his head through and see that the bottom bolts both have their knobs pressed away from him.

Keeping one half of the window twisted open, he

reaches down for the wedge and presses it down into the door. Then, reaching down with the knife, he levers both bottom bolts' knobs away from the wood.

Out of reach of his fingers—the gap only allowing his arm to reach in so far—he uses the pliers to pull up the bolts. Now both sides of the window swing open.

Martin collects up his tools, wraps them in the long strip of rag, zips them back into his jacket pocket, and is about to step into the bedroom when he notices the mud on his trainers. He heels them off. (Had the knife, wedges and tin not succeeded, he was simply going to hammer a hole through the double-glazing. Not having had to do that, he doesn't want to leave any tell-tale signs.)

The bedroom carpet prickles through his damp socks.

Although Martin tells himself that he is positive, with the lights being out, that the man has left the house, another voice asks: What if the man has simply taken himself back to bed? Or gone out for a walk? In this weather? Who can tell? Even now, he could be watching Martin from the woods ...

Martin's heart hammers are slamming as he looks around. But outside the window, beyond the dark overhang, are just the diagonal, silver rain and shiny, wet trees. And he remembers the blackness of these windows seen from across the way. No, he isn't being watched.

He opens the bedroom door to the inner hall.

The hallway is dark. Grey daylight comes from behind him and from the stairwell. Windblown rain pecks at the upstairs windows. Before stepping out into the corridor, Martin pulls a bedroom chair across and positions it to make sure that the door stays open behind him.

Not knowing what he'll find—he has imagined the boys in everything from shackles to a drugged stupor—Martin opens the door opposite.

It's an office—computer screens, keyboards, fax machine, telephones. Two blue swivel chairs on black castors. He spots the double-glazed skylight that he'd anticipated, with globs of rain on it, a shelf of business and financial directories, and a shelf of box files.

The next room is a bedroom: double bed, bathroom en suite. In the next, smaller room is a single bed, shower en suite. There is nowhere else downstairs for the boys to be hidden—apart from the door into the store, and Martin is certain they won't have been moved there. And he has already looked in through the double windows of all the other bedrooms downstairs.

Pausing to take a couple of deep breaths, he starts slowly up the stairs past the rain-spotted round window. His socks are slippery on the bare wooden steps.

Upstairs, apart from the large open-plan kitchen and another bathroom, is one large room partially divided by a wall. The wall is covered with framed photographs. A table, with a notebook and pen on it, is by the far corner window.

On either side of the wall is a higgledy-piggledy assortment of expensive sofas and chairs, a scattering of magazines, a large television, a bookshelf and a stereo unit.

A door goes through to the garage above the boat store. It's empty: no boys.

Another squall bumps against the big windows. Irresolute, Martin tells himself that there's nothing here, that it'd be best to leave. But he was so sure that the boys were here, that he would find them here. Now he doesn't know what to think.

"So where are they?" he asks the strange house.

The trees on either side of the drive are being lashed back and forth by the gale. He tells himself that he'd better leave: with all that chaotic movement out there he won't notice the car or the man coming, nor will he hear anything above the noise of the storm.

Once more he goes quickly around the house, opens cupboards and wardrobes (no visible trapdoors), and even pulls open the door to the boat-store, breaking webs. Finally he steps outside and ties his trainers back on. Unwrapping his knife he closes the window pair, both bottom bolts balanced so that they will drop into place when he pushes the window closed, the latch raised. This he does, withdraws his knife, and gives the frames a shake. The windows cannot be pulled open.

Taking a small jar of brown woodstain from his pocket, Martin dribbles a bit down over the scratched wood and works it in with his thumb. He does the same to the windowframe he'd splintered last time.

Finally, the rag-wrapped tools zipped into his pocket, Martin runs off into the tail-end of a shower. He keeps on running.

Around the other side of the lake he slips and falls. Stopped, he lays there, and can feel his chest inflating and deflating. A waterbird makes a noise down near the lake. The house across the way is still and dark. Leaves drip. The wind shimmies the glinting leaves of a horse chestnut.

Lying there, the wet rising cold up through his clothes, Martin feels helpless—and feels watched. From the dark between the trees, or from behind, someone, or something, is watching him: cameras hidden in knot holes? The shiny, wet trees themselves sensing his presence?

Martin kneels up, defiant: let them watch. He knows, knows with a certainty that puzzles him, that the two boys are here.

So private and quiet is this place, so out of the world, so ordered but wild, that it feels as though a spell has been put upon it. Green-white lichen furs the branches, while moss and ivy creep up over old stumps. Time transforms things here. Have the trespassing boys been turned into something else? Frogs? Snakes? The watching trees?

A practical man at heart, Martin tells himself not to be daft, unsticks himself from the ground, shivers and plods on.

As soon as Steve hears Martin's voice, its lack of exhilaration, and the absence of any urgent command, he knows that Martin hasn't found the two boys.

Steve had envisioned himself trotting off to fetch the van, driving back, helping the boys down from the roof of the van, all of them laughing, hugging each other, and him driving them all home, at last having done one thing worthwhile in his son's eyes. Instead, he watches Martin, with mud all up his clothes, and clumsy with tiredness, letting himself down onto the board.

Steve takes the board from him, helps him to slide the ladder into the van, and has to ask, "No sign?"

"Not a fucking thing."

They drive down through the wet, green fields towards the glistening slate roofs of Estley.

"So, what now?" Steve says.

"Got no fuckin' option," Martin says. "Let the police know."

As they cross the road in Estley, Steve thinks he sees Sweets' Mercedes. And, thinking he may get told off for using the van on a Saturday, he suddenly resents having been made to use it. "So where are they?"

"Up there. Sure of it. Where else?"

"A million places. I should've listened to Mary, and gone to the police straightaway."

"She's gonna go now. So what the fuck?"

# 19

The holy earth is overspread with leaves,
Wind crosses a thousand miles of autumn fields.

**Tesshu** (1879-1939)

Sister Clare, this wet afternoon I want to tell you about
religion ... about our parents' religion ...
    It depended on the film they were in at the time.
Remember the arguments when he was doing a biopic of
Nietsche and she was Joan of Arc? Since then, and before,
they've been everything from Californian Buddhists to
Holders-of-the-Faith-Against-Dracula, or some such evil.
The latest is, he's an animist—Cro-Magnon Man from
Cloud-Cuckoo Land.
    Remember our christening, sister? My christening us?
    We were about seven or eight, staying in that stately
pile while they did the costume drama. There was that long
rectangular pond with the shell fountain at the end.
    I took you out there at night when the moon was full.
I remember I felt very brave taking all my clothes off
outdoors and climbing down into the water. But it wasn't
nearly as deep as I'd thought. I had to kneel to hide my
sex—our difference. Then I had to lean right over the
water—to obliterate the moon's white face—so that I could
see just you looking back up at me.
    I'd been practising it for days, had some mumbo-

jumbo ready, had wanted to give us different names. Our names. I was to be Blackthorn—you, Willow. And, so named, I splashed myself into you.

But it was so very cold and I was shivering so much I couldn't get myself dressed. Tiptoeing back across the lawn—with those tiny little steps the naked take—teeth chattering, looking for the quickest way back indoors, I forgot all about the alarm lights. Suddenly there was all this shrieking and laughing.

I didn't tell them why—I knew they'd have thought it was 'cute'. Or I'd have been packed off to the nearest and latest child psychology expert. "Wasn't deep enough to swim," was all I told them. Our mother played the concerned-about-my-health parent. Our father was Falstaffianly manful about his son's boyish devilry.

I get talked to about religion a lot now—about the loss of religion, the loss of a loved one leading to a loss of faith.

Religions are all about death. In my teens I saw that death-centred religions like Christianity—with its emphasis on crucifixion, on the sought death, on the celebrated deaths of martyrs, and with its glamorising of the various means of death—simply used all those past deaths to justify all its latterday death-making actions. In any religion, in Islam too, its adherents do not defy death, they actively seek it. With their expectations of an eternity, they seek the passage of death, while denying the actuality of death.

I was still in my teens when I gave up trying to make sense of the nonsense of religion. (Contrary to all their obsessiveness about death, you were there, I felt you there, and you were dead, neverborn.) So I didn't understand. I decided then that I wanted neither to live by reason alone—I would never have sufficient information—nor to give up my free will to religious forces—shamanistic and mysterious—beyond my knowing. I would live, I decided, by a simple understanding of how things really work, an understanding which would have to include an awareness, an admission, of my being unable to know how all things work.

Over the years I've come to see that all religious types get caught up in a paradox, a kind of two-way tug: between recognising and shouting out the truth, and wanting to belong to the religious group. Belonging requires conformity, and conformity to any creed will impede any real search for truth, for the unanticipated truth.

Now I have come to see that what we seek in religion is not One-ness, is not The Truth, but is the strength of mind to accept, for more than occasional moments, the whole of life honestly perceived. That strength of mind goes far beyond the everyday, beyond self-congratulation, and so it is hard to build. Like muscles, strength of mind needs to be worked at regularly. It is also a strength which requires struggle, which needs to test itself through the holding of false notions. Strength of mind needs to find itself often disenchanted with itself. It is a constant process, rather than a state of being.

Live long enough, sister, I decided, and you'll watch all ideals become, not only corrupt in themselves, but a force for corruption.

All our minds are flawed, sister. We cannot achieve true objectivity. Look at the tricks the mind plays. Like, for instance, when we've been ill, and afterwards we try to recall exactly how very ill we felt. (And you are still there, sister, I feel you there, and you are dead, neverborn.)

In the end, sister, any desire for objectivity has to be more important than any objective truth, than any transient truth achieved. Any desire for truth has to be more important than The Truth, or whatever else religionists want to call it.

I know this sister. I know that I deceive myself. You are dead, sister Clare; and yet I know that you are not dead, sister Clare, not while I am still alive.

All that, however, is religion as I perceive it. For others, I have come to see that a system of unprovable beliefs is important—both to the individual and to society.

Fay needed to believe, like some people need to believe in magic. Even though they know there is sleight of hand involved, still they are happy to enjoy the illusion of magic. Some are not happy unless they think they know the exact mechanics of the trick. But both still want to believe in magic.

A god, any god, is but a focus of belief. When—like Fay—you cannot make sense of this world of people, then to be told what is right and what is wrong comes as a relief. Except that, out of this social confusion, fascists can come. That's when the confused find out they've been obeying all the wrong rules; they will be punished for that obedience.

As a child, as a teenager, religions offered me belonging, only asking me to be good. But, so various had been my upbringing, that I did not know what 'good' was. I also carried within me a million little meannesses known only to myself—and to you. Our 'baptism' had been meant to cleanse me of some of those 'sins'.

And what were those 'sins'? They were small, spiteful acts to children who had disappointed me. (They weren't you.) Those 'sins' bothered my sleep. My sleep is no longer bothered by such dreams. Now I sleep well. But I do not wake refreshed.

That is a lie. And not a lie. I still dream. I do not wake refreshed. But it is not the dreams that have bothered me.

More a lack of restorative rest.

Dreams, I have decided, because they are like a scene watched, because they are like something experienced, can take on a false importance. We try hard to remember them, to decipher them, because we think they're important. But if they were that important, they'd be easy to remember.

Logic is confounded here.

I do still have a horror of dreams. And I know I dream, that I slip at the close of my eyes into past lives that are incompatible with the present. I'm relieved to wake in the morning and not be able to recall any of those dreams. Even so, I am exhausted by them.

There was a time, sister, when my dreams were so vivid they were like another reality. Remember that dream journal I kept? I lost myself pattern-seeking in that chaos of dreams.

As you well know, sister, mind-made things are none the less real for being mind-made.

Just now, sister, I found another bedroom window tampered with. I almost missed it—they made a better job of covering up the damage with some kind of wood stain— though the window's top catches were left undone.

There is nothing missing in the house, not that I can see. Nor can I see any definite marks. I'm convinced, though, that they've been in here: cupboard doors ajar that weren't left ajar, and doors closed that weren't fully closed before.

I can find no bombs, nor any bugs. A hidden bomb in the house I'll take my chances with—it'd have to be big to blow the whole house up, therefore it wouldn't be easily hidden. And if they've planted bugs, they won't hear much in this house—where I live alone, where the only person I talk to is you. Nor will reading this help them—not only is my ordinary handwriting near illegible, this is written in our usual code.

Small reassurance, though. I get the feeling they're playing with me, setting me up for the kill.

They're waiting, I'm convinced of it, wanting something from me beforehand. What?

I know well, sister, the mechanics of killing. I know too that once you've started down that path, there's no knowing where, or with whom, it will stop.

I just wish I knew exactly how they were getting into the garden.

# 20

Mary wants to phone.

"You'll just get fobbed off," Tina tells her, taking charge.

So they catch the bus up to town, both of them scanning the stop-go shopping pavements for signs of their boys. If either catch sight of them it will make all this, all these last few days, unthinkably silly, and it will save them from the next step.

Neither see them.

Mary, gagging nervous, follows Tina into the white brick police station.

Tina is wearing jeans. The undisguised width of Tina's bum embarrasses Mary—as if it was her own on show.

Tina has caught the confused glances, knows that she and nervous Mary can never become friends. (No-one feels that they are liked for themselves, only for what they represent, and Tina knows that she represents nothing to Mary now—save trouble and loss.)

Through the small-paned door is a kind of shop counter with a flap, and to one side of it a red, padded bench. With its glass panel slid open, it reminds Mary of the Council offices. Except that here there's a young, ginger-haired policeman looking at them from behind the counter.

Mary feels so weak and nervous that she has to sit on the bench. Tina, irritated by this unexpected desertion—it was Mary who wanted to come here—frowns down at her.

The ginger policeman lifts his eyebrows and smiles.

Mary wants to slip onto the floor, crawl to the door, slide back outside, and make as if she has never been here.

Mary wants to tell Tina to stop bossing her.

Mary wants all this not to have happened.

Mary wants not to have come here. Although she's been saying all week she should come here—coming here, telling them, will make Dan's absence too real. Being here will make him really 'missing'—not just from home, but missing from everywhere.

"Come on!" Tina whispers and taps her leg with the side of her shoe.

Mary wants the police to find her Dan. What if they already have some idea?

"Can I help you?" the policeman finally asks them.

Tina turns to him as Mary, clutching herself up the wall, stands.

"Our boys have gone missing," they say together.

The young policeman makes a half-nod to accept that information. Now both women press their bellies against the counter.

"How long they been missing?" the policeman asks, looking from one to the other.

"Four, five ..." Tina starts.

"Six days!" Mary nearly shouts. She feels as if she's going to faint. She wants to sit down again but thinks the policeman might think she's not interested.

They watch the policeman's large freckled hand write '6 days' on a small notepad.

"How old are your sons?"

"Fifteen," Mary says.

"Simon's sixteen this month."

"And they haven't been seen for almost a week?"

"No."

"Either of them ever gone missing before?"

"No."

"Not even for a night?"

The two women glance almost to one another.

"They got into trouble last year—you arrested them," Mary hears herself gabble. "That's how we knew where they were then. You arrested them. But they weren't missing. They weren't missing then."

"I'm sorry," the policeman acknowledges Mary's agitation. "I have to establish the facts here—that's all. I just wanted to be sure, in my own mind, what you meant by 'missing'."

"Not home." Mary says. She can feel tears. "Not here."

"I understand," he says. "Now if you can give me their names, their full names ..."

Mary hadn't expected this—this sympathy. She had expected someone older and brusque to brush her aside, not this solicitous noting down of details—date of birth, address. She recalls how last time Dan had joked at the back of the court with a grey-bearded policeman. Dan wouldn't tell her what it was about.

This ginger policeman does not react, by pause or squint, to their living in Hambrook. He goes on to write down the boys' school, and what both boys were wearing when last seen. He asks Tina and Mary their own names.

"Are you both married?"

Mary and Tina nod when looked at.

"Your present husbands are the boys' fathers? What I mean is, there's no likelihood, if you were separated, of the boys going off secretly to stay with one of their fathers?"

"No," Tina declares aggressively. (Both women were

shaking their heads, waiting for him to finish.) "Their
fathers are as worried as us."

"Why didn't you report it sooner? Six days seems ..."

"Well, we thought ..." Tina doesn't know what she
thought. "Just the one night, we thought. You know what
boys are like ..."

"We thought they might be in trouble with you."
Mary was careful to say 'we'. She doesn't want Tina to think
that she is trying to blame her for the delay.

"What kind of trouble?"

"Cars. Stealing cars." Mary says, chin forward, not
looking at Tina. "My husband didn't want to be the one
who dropped them in it."

"Names aren't familiar. No." The policeman shakes
his head. "Hold on a sec—I'll check."

Mary and Tina wait, bellies still pressed against the
counter, while the young policeman goes to the phone at
the back of the room. Although facing them, he talks with
his head down into the phone. His ginger hair is clipped and
gelled. Tina and Mary can't hear exactly what he's saying,
but catch enough of his words to guess the gist of it.

Another, older policeman comes in and bends down,
looking for something in one of the cupboards.

"Next shelf down," the ginger policeman says, putting
his hand over the mouthpiece.

He removes the hand again to answer some questions.
The other policeman looks through a file of plastic sheets,
takes one and puts the others back. Then the ginger
policeman puts the phone down, comes over to the counter.

"A detective will be out to see you shortly. If you care
to take a seat?" His large hand indicates the red padded
bench.

"Has he heard anything?"

"He didn't say."

Mary and Tina sit not quite touching on the red bench. The ginger policeman answers the phone. It is to do with something that he sent off two weeks ago. The detective doesn't come.

"Never thought about that," Mary says. "Suppose it must happen a lot."

"What?"

"Kids going off to see their fathers, or their mothers, if they're divorced."

"Yeah," Tina says. "But you'd have some idea then, wouldn't you? You could check. They wouldn't be missing then, would they?"

"No," Mary says. "Suppose not."

A door beside the counter opens. A young man with floppy brown hair and a blue shirt smiles at them,

"Mrs Thurlow? Mrs Flinthorn?" Tina and Mary stand. "If you'd like to come this way ..."

He leads them along a cream-painted corridor—which reminds Tina of school, Mary of hospital. The high room into which he shows them has frosted windows, a table and four soft chairs, one hard chair, phone sockets and computer points. There's a red phone on the floor in the corner, but no computers.

"Take a seat," he says gesturing to the soft chairs. He sits himself on the hard chair and arranges a large writing pad on the table in front of him. The boys' names are already written, in sloping capitals, upon it.

"Sorry to make you answer the same questions again, but the desk officer has to keep his notes and I've got to keep mine. It's the way it is these days. Never know when you're going to get sued by some hopeful. Now ..."

Dates of birth are given again, addresses, schools ...

and this time a detailed physical description. With this, the two women help one another:

"What would you say—brown?"

"Looks older, don't he, Dan?"

All these details—distinguishing features, scars, tattoos—he enters on a preprinted form.

These details—each distinguishing feature—has Mary sniffing back her tears. The detective, to allow the two mothers time to compose themselves, looks back through the forms and notes laid out before him.

Now both women, despite their distress, are ready to answer more questions. They are not used to silence, to time being taken. Practical women they are—both liking to get on with whatever's to hand. Both women, now, want to get on with this interview.

"When were they last seen?"

"Friday?" Mary says. "Before last."

"You sound uncertain. Who saw them?"

"Nathan," Tina says. "My youngest."

The detective has started writing.

"He's thirteen," Tina tells him. "Got his head shaved."

"Where did he see them?"

"Climbing over a wall into a garden."

The detective looks at her. Tina glances towards Mary. Neither speak.

"And this is why you didn't come to us sooner?"

Both women, eyes reddened, nod.

"Fair enough. Where is this garden?"

"In the woods up above Estley."

"Know the name of the house?"

"No. But it's the one that belongs to that gangster. The one whose family got killed."

The blue-shirted detective continues writing, raises

his head slightly to signify that he has heard.

"So what do you think has happened to them?"

"We don't know. Don't even know if they're still there. But ..."

"You think they're still there?"

"No ..." Tina says. "Well, no. No, we don't know. That's why we come to you.".

"Their fathers," Mary presses forward to speak, not turning to Tina, "have been up to have a look. They found a fire where they got over." Mary lets go a sob and sinks back.

"The boys' fathers have also been in this garden?"

"Climbed the wall ... yeah," Tina says. Mary and Tina have been made to promise not to mention Martin's breaking into the house. "They reckon the boys could be in the house still. Being kept there."

"Hold on." The detective lifts his hand. "What are you saying here?" He looks at Mary, "That you think they've been killed? That they've been burnt on a fire?"

"His own children were burnt alive."

"And you—you're saying," he says to Tina, "you think they're being held captive in the house?"

"Where else are they?"

The detective sits back, away from the table, and looks from Mary to Tina. He moves the forms and papers around on the table, and drums his fingers. Then he stands and says, "I'm going to have to consult a colleague. Won't be a minute." He stops at the door, "Like a cup of tea?" Both women partly turn to gesture 'please'. "I'll send some in."

Their being offered tea means to them that they are being taken seriously. Letting that sink in, they wait.

Tina wants to tell Mary she hadn't realised that she thought they were dead. And now she wants to clutch onto this other woman and for them both to weep out their woe.

Not, though, in this dangerous place. Instead, she whispers, "Marty's gonna be mad at me mentioning them in there."

"How else we supposed to tell 'em?"

They go silent as the door opens. The ginger policeman from the desk brings in a tray with two white mugs and a glass sugar bowl, a spoon sticking out of the sugar.

"Didn't know if either of you took sugar."

"No, thank you," both women say. He takes the sugar bowl back out with the tray.

Holding their mugs in both hands, the two women blow and drink, and wait. The blue-shirted detective comes back with an older, stouter man in a dark suit, white shirt and dark tie. The young detective introduces him, "This is Detective Inspector Lemprian."

Inspector Lemprian has a map with him. He unfolds it on the table, swivels it around for the two women to look at. Their mugs held in both hands, they rise from their low chairs and stoop to peer at the map.

"Where's this gangster's house?"

"Here," Mary says. She had made Steve show her on the map at home.

"And you honestly believe your son is being kept in this house?"

Mary and Tina lower their backsides again onto the low chairs.

"Where else is he?" Tina says.

Inspector Lemprian looks down on Tina and Mary. He has no expression. Mary thinks, because of his black hair and his blank face, he must be Chinese. But he doesn't sound Chinese.

"Your son, thieving little sod that he is," Inspector Lemprian says to Tina, "has probably got himself locked in somewhere. Not very good at thieving is he? If I remember rightly, he smashed up the last car he nicked."

This is the reaction that Mary had anticipated from the police. She sets her mouth straight and brings her knees together, while beside her she can feel Tina puffing herself up.

"What do you know?" Mary says in a low and stubborn voice.

"I know your son is a thief."

"OK," Mary nods, not wanting to argue with this man. "OK. I know my boy's no angel. But I know he would have come home if he could. I know that. And you lot here would've known about any crashed cars."

The Inspector continues to look at her, then shifts his gaze to Tina, who's about to speak. He says first, "Why'd you let your son hang out with a no-good like Dan Flinthorn?"

"They're friends," Tina puts on her fighting front. "Been friends a long time. Good for each other, I'd have said."

"So what're they doing climbing into somebody else's garden?"

"Garden? You seen the size of the place? It's got a lake in the middle with a fucking boat on it. 'Garden'—bollocks."

"How do you know it's got a lake?"

"My husband climbed over—to look for our sons."

"That's the way your family thinks is it? Why didn't he just go to the front door and ask?"

"Are you joking? He's a fucking gangster. Our boys broke in there."

"Now you're asking us to go in there."

"You're the police," Tina grunts. "Unless, like Marty

says ..."

"Marty says what?" The Inspector has raised both his straight black eyebrows.

"I was going to say, unless you're frightened of him too." (Tina wasn't going to say that. She was going to say, 'Unless, like Marty says, you're in his pay'. But now she was aware of Mary beside her letting out a long sigh, and saw no point in antagonising this boring suit unnecessarily.)

The inspector slowly brings his hands, palms together, pointing outwards from his belly. The two women look at the joined hands. "This is what is going to happen," he says. "I'm going to send officers round to interview your husbands. About exactly what they've seen in this garden. I will also be sending around an officer from our juvenile section to interview your other son. I daresay she will be accompanied by a Social Worker. If you agree to this, your sons will be registered as missing as from now, and their descriptions will be circulated throughout the country. We shall also begin investigations locally. Do you agree?"

Both women, as if hypnotised by the fast flow of words, now slowly nod.

The Inspector's hands come apart, are lifted palms outwards, "Fine. You will both be required to make individual statements. But before that let's go over this once again ..."

# 21

Sister, your death—the endless possibilities of your might-have-been-ness—I have never come to terms with.

My own death is a simple future fact, easily acceptable. It will happen. Not now, dramatically. That expectation has changed: I am old now and the biochemical machine below is playing up: tubes are losing their elasticity, the whole body is losing its power of recovery. One of these days I know I won't wake up.

My own death does not now appal nor frighten me. Which is only natural—the older one gets the more familiar one gets with pain. Being familiar with pain, the less afraid of pain we get, the more pain, therefore, we can tolerate. So the prospect of death, of becoming dead and pain-free, comes to seem a piece of cake. (But, I confess, I am coming to fear the cold. Cold feels like death creeping up on me.)

Fay's death frightened me far more than yours or the prospect of mine.

Fay was such a big part of my life—I hadn't realised how big, until she was dead. (Understand this, sister—when Fay was alive she wasn't you, was not in any way your replacement.)

Her life made sense of mine. My life now has no sense to it. Fay's death tore a whole piece of my life from me. It wounded me—fatally?

In her dying, Fay took with her my last wonder of death. And she left behind this blank knowledge, this knowledge of blankness—to know and never tell. Tell what?

I have almost died many times. A man's life—all of it—is open to chance, is dependent on the choices that others make, is prey even to the fickleness of microbes. The slush pump will one day stop.

I was shot once, been stabbed twice, and I have risked my all several times. I have—almost deliberately—put my own life in danger, have dared others take it, and was exhilarated by the risk. Such alarms, such close shaves, made me prize the commonplace, caused the very air to become valuable, every brick in a wall to take on importance. So too all the trees, leaves, grains of sand ...

Dying is different from killing. The deaths of others do not upset me. I say this not because I am a monster, that I take delight in deaths: I do not. (I am not one of those who buys murder magazines, reads horror novels, true-crime stories, or real-life murder periodicals.) Killing has always been to me nothing more than the removal of an obstacle.

Nor am I a politician: I do not savour the power-plays that cause the incidental deaths of hundreds.

Nor have my killings been a spillage over of violence into murder. My violence has always served a purpose. (Like the armies that everyone's taxes pay for.)

Nor have my killings had their root in sensuality, in the seeking of ever more exciting sensual experiences, which seek ultimate satisfaction in murder. I am innocent of that.

My aim always has been simply to get where I want by the quickest and most direct route. And if somebody has been in the way of my getting what I want, then I have killed them—or, lately, had them killed.

What I want now, for instance, is peace and quiet. These latest intruders are putting themselves in the way of my peace and quiet. (Maybe it's because of them that I can feel death hunting me down.) Once I find out who they are, I will have them removed, permanently: end of story—their story.

Your story, sister, never began. My story, consequently, can never be complete.

Death cannot be the final result of a life. Our death has to affect the lives of those closest to us—as an absence. Or, at the very least, it will affect the person who finds our body. Which is why so many of my clients have difficulty accepting suicides. They feel the death was deliberately willed upon them, so they themselves were made the victim.

Ollie and Mal's lives, purely on the strength of the money they'll inherit, will change dramatically on my death. Will their precious marriages survive that dramatic change? What effect will it have on their children, and on their children's attitude towards them?

I am not trying—in my will—to influence their futures. I have been parentally even-handed. Ollie might well think of himself as deserving of more. Who can tell? Who knows what legacies of bitterness I might leave: brother blaming sister, bearing grudges against nephews and nieces, sister conniving and conspiring to cheat brother ... Who knows?

No parent can know how their death will affect their children. My children might be ecstatic that, not only are they shot of the shame of me, they are both instantly rich into the bargain.

Or they might, both of them caught up in their own lives, be indifferent to my passing. At the other extreme— and I will have woefully misread my elder two if this were to be the case—they could be so overcome with grief that they will want to join me in death.

Nor is there any way of predicting the effect of our

death on the greater world. News of our death—if it makes the papers—could be on the same page as a male pin-up, predictions for a marathon, or a campaign for bicycle safety, or lost among adverts for car tyres and cut-price bedlinen. We are simply dead, gone, finished: the world has other cares.

That is not to say that our lives are of no consequence. No life, once begun, ever ends. Even yours sister, which never truly began.

I've often wondered, sister, if I have created you as my anchor for when I quit this bodily life. (I am kidding myself—I know that when we quit, we quit: I have seen life leave with that last, long sigh, and believe me, nothing remains.) But in the middle of the night sometimes, counting the years on my way to join the dead, I worry— sometimes silly worries—will there be any room left? The dead are so many ...

One thing is for certain, sister: when dead, I won't be alone. But this is no reassurance. I hate crowds.

This lengthy consideration of death, sister, this consideration of my dying, does not mean that I am going to spend the rest of my life sitting here planning my funeral. That would be to live my life negatively. And so much of it, already, mainly because of you, sister, has not been positive.

What is 'here', sister? These words? Time's fixative? A vanity. Which is all our parents care about, sister—how they would be judged by the future. Sure they talked about making changes in the present—they talked of doing this or that, of bringing something 'to the public eye'—but that wasn't why they did any such thing. They did it because they wanted to be remembered by the future for having done it.

Here, this piece of paper, is not my bid for ownership

of the future. This is in code. It will not be seen by the
future. This writing will only, I hope, change me, change
my present.

Can't say, though, I've yet noticed any change in
myself yet.

Death, in a drama, can define a life. Hence the
temptation to use it as the only definition of a life—its
manner of, or approach to, its death. But death is only one
of the defining characteristics of a real life. More important
is the world in which the life is lived: the social climate,
political atmosphere, competing religions, philosophical
preoccupations, language and machines used, people
known, ideas and superstitions held, what that person
believed their achievements to be, their disappointments,
their aspirations.

This slot we've had in time, sister, this parcel of life
that has been ours ... I could as easily have been an artisan
or an assassin three thousand years ago in Egypt, or a
single-minded survivor three thousand years hence. Yet here
I am now, wandering through a garden of my own making,
with my fifty-plus years so far. (I paused on my walk to jot
that down and a red admiral butterfly mistook the white of
the notepad for a flower. That is life—in all its delicate trial-
and-error beauty.)

Death, sister, death is not to be celebrated. No-one
takes photos at funerals. Yet remembrance is supposed to be
what it's all about.

There will be no shrines built to me. I'll be the
soonest forgotten. I have been, after all, a hundred-carat
shit.

# 22

This report is in four parts:
1) INTELLIGENCE
2) ACTION TAKEN
3) REPORTS
4) EVALUATION/SUBJECTIVE ASSESSMENT
Author of Report—DI Frank Lemprian

1) INTELLIGENCE

On the afternoon of Saturday 8th September two women approached the station desk officer. They identified themselves as Tina Thurlow and Mary Flinthorn, and they said that they wanted to report their sons—Simon Thurlow and Daniel Flinthorn—missing. Both boys are 15 years old. Both boys had last been seen, for certain, on 30th August.

The two women were subsequently interviewed together by DC Neil Bradshaw. He asked why there was a delay in reporting these two minors missing. (The school term had started the previous Tuesday—the two boys were therefore truant. It should also be noted here that, although they were just beginning their last year of schooling, taken together the two boys already had convictions for stealing from shops, stealing pushbikes, for receiving stolen goods, for criminal damage, and for vehicle theft.)

Both mothers first said that they had delayed reporting their sons missing because they didn't want to get them into more trouble. Upon further questioning, however, Mary Flinthorn said that they knew where their sons had gone and their husbands had been trying to find them. Tina Thurlow said that her youngest son, 13 year old Nathaniel Thurlow, had seem the two older boys climb over a wall into the gardens of Upper Estley House.

The two fathers had then gone to see if the two boys were still over the other side of that wall. They found that the branches the boys had used to climb over the wall had been cut off. So they climbed over by other means. (A ladder? Neither the mothers, nor subsequently the fathers, would say.) That day, and on subsequent days, thinking that the two boys might be hiding there, the two fathers—Steven Flinthorn and Martin Thurlow—searched the extensive grounds of Upper Estley House for the two boys. Unable to find them they came to suspect that the owner may have caught them trespassing and done something to them. The mothers, becoming increasingly alarmed, came to us.

*Confidential (separate sheet)*
When DC Bradshaw consulted me about the missing boys—I've had contact with both boys in the past—I recalled National Directive S92/600B4 concerning Upper Estley House. To wit—'Any legitimate reason to search this property and make record of documentary evidence shall be expedited, with the assurance of any such comprehensive search being funded from national resources.' Standing Committee On Organised Crime. A missing persons with description of the two boys as 'at risk' was issued, and, on the strength of a possible murder investigation, and as soon as both fathers had independently confirmed that the address was as the mothers had said, National Directive S92/600B4 was actioned.

# 23

Sister ... dear sister, I have just got back from 'the office' and now I've got somebody else's problems inside my head.

I want to shout and growl.

I suppose if Fay were alive I'd confide all these curious stories to her, not be sat here confiding them to you. Fay would have been interested in these people and their problems. But Fay's death is why, is how, I got the job. (And there was nothing I could tell Fay about my other work. Hadn't dared tell her. Each small, reported act would have lain like a strangeness between us.)

Would Fay have let me tell her about these people? It's all supposed to be as confidential as the confessional. I doubt, sister, if it's a breach of confidentiality my telling you. Even then ... even then, I have so convinced myself of the need for absolute confidentiality—to believe it myself and thus convince them that I can be trusted—that that belief won't let me now tell you their very ordinary secrets, won't let me talk even to you about their life dilemmas, other than in the most general terms.

I go there, sister, I sit there, and I listen to them talking themselves into their new reality.

The unthinkable has happened to them, and I am there as the world's representative to acknowledge the new truth of their lives. My presence alone, my being sat there opposite them, says, "Yes, this is what has happened."

Many can't accept, because they are fools—fools who

never gave a thought to life, to its variety, to its myriad possibilities. Trauma has left these mortals without a self-image.

They're exactly the kind of people I blazed against when I was young: those who accepted—as the real world—every contradiction thrown at them. And here I am, now, 'accepting' them.

Some I do feel truly sorry for. And that sympathy has led me to realise that, though I may identify with the wounded and the damaged, it is only with those who have kept their scars secret.

With the majority of them I pretend sympathy—to cover the contempt I have for their thoughtless existence. The same contempt, I suspect, that a comedian has for his audience—watching them laugh again and again at the same old gags and antics. The comedian presses the switches, the audience machine laughs and claps. Behavioural responses. In my 'office' I provoke them, gently, to tears. People always feel better for a good cry.

My contempt, in this job, isn't reserved for the clients. One look through any client's notes will show you how self-congratulatory the caring profession is. If a patient lives, it's all credit to the carers. Should anyone die, then it was beyond the carers' powers. I have no powers.

I have no powers of healing. I am simply there to listen, to accept. But I do try, through my questions, not to let them fool themselves.

There is a state of mind, sister, that believes 'Life would be perfect if only ...' With my questions I try to bring them to the knowledge that perfection is impossible. Nor is there any absolute truth. (Truth, sister, is other people's fictions that we choose to believe.)

Lately I have been given to wondering why we seek to

calm, to reassure everyone. Some people need to be upset.

Lately too I have come of the mind that some people do not deserve our help and our time. These are the people who need a 'problem' in their life, who would be nothing without a 'problem'. They will therefore make some aspect of their otherwise unremarkable life into a problem.

With most of those I listen to, they seek to make a career out of their grief. And I am left, sat there with the futility of trying to change a fixed mind, with the frustration of being unable to impart what I know, of being unable to prevent these people deluding themselves.

I've got one especially infuriating woman who seems pathologically incapable of seeing reality. She was the driver of the car in which her husband was killed. She was drunk. His family now despise her. And she refuses to believe that they can despise her because of what she has done. She believes that someone—unnamed—has put them up to it.

Where did this woman come by the expectation, by no means grounded in her other life experiences, that the whole world will always be friendly towards her? I know that, one day soon, I'm going to blow up at her, and vomit the cold truth over her. And she will leave in tears asking, why, sob, why is the world always so hateful towards her?

This I have learnt, sister, that all of us defensively, for the sake of our personal integrity, assume ourselves to be complete, to be a whole, to be a self-constructed person. The older we get, the greater is the assumption, and the harder it is for us to open ourselves up to new knowledge— to something outside ourselves. No, I take that back: the assimilation of new knowledge is easy enough, providing it doesn't threaten our identity, doesn't threaten our constructed image of ourselves. It is the cancellation of our own supposed completeness that is hard.

My clients are sent to me because they have found themselves in a new reality. This new reality has estranged my clients, has dislocated them. What they thought was real, isn't. Thus their relationship to that reality isn't real either. But still they want to belong—somewhere. To be allowed to belong, they have to think themselves well thought of—by someone. But wanting something good to be said about them can lead people to act in the most bizarre fashion.

Sister, I am an intimate of the mad. Of course many are suspicious of me. They see me as yet another therapist. They have come to me via psychologists and various other analysts—professionals who build whole theories of their clients' lives upon single words uttered, or even on one peculiar gesture. Such observant, such learned people are dangerous to have conversations with. Who knows what new conclusions they might reach, and what new treatments they might try as a result?

I have to convince these clients, these victims—before they start to talk—that I just listen, that I report to no-one—not even to God, I told a Catholic. I tell them that they can say what they like to me and it will go no further.

And it nearly always works. Not because of who I am. There could be someone else sat in my place, saying the same thing. No, it works—like any branch of psychology works, like all religions and systems of jurisprudence work—because of the human compulsion to tell the truth. Even when the truth bears witness against themselves. (Like these letters to you, sister. Though I don't think even I've got to the truth yet.)

I find the obsessions of the knowing-themselves-to-be-mad, their unsociableness, easier than the unspent grief of the 'normal' repressed. As you and I know, sister, a little

craziness every so often can keep you sane—if all that it
does, is stop you taking the familiar for granted. That same
craziness can also keep you alive. It has kept me alive.

Consequently, from this moment on, I am going to
abandon all my habits, act on contrary impulse, cut cards,
flip coins, and roll dice for random plans. I will not be prey
to predictability. I will not be an easy target for those who
are hunting me down. I will trick them into revealing
themselves.

# 24

Where there are humans
you'll find flies,
and Buddhas.

**Issa** (1763-1827)

2) ACTION TAKEN

A search warrant applied for and issued, a team to search
Upper Estley House was assembled on the morning of
Monday 10th September.

At 5:32am, an electrician diverted the supply to the
gate locks, enabling us to approach the house without giving
advance warning. Once all officers were in position, we
roused the owner from his bed. (He was observed to come
straight from his bed to the front door.) He gave the
appearance of being puzzled, but readily agreed to allowing
us to search his house and his land for the two missing boys.

The house search was conducted by the forensic team.
I engaged the owner while co-ordinating the external
searches.

The task of the outside non-specialised search team
was to trawl through the grounds. The specialist ground
teams employed a subterranean-imager, checking for any
recently disturbed earth. The indoors forensic team also
went out later to take samples from the two recent bonfires.

The helicopter made infra-red maps of the property, plus a black-and-white photographic survey, plus a digitised image map.

Divers performed a fingertip search of the lake bed.

Throughout the day the owner co-operated with the enquiry, answered all questions asked of him and, although told he could if he wished, he made no attempt to contact his solicitor. Apart from when, accompanied, he got himself washed and dressed, he remained with me or another officer in the upper part of the house—which consists of one long room partially divided lengthways by a single wall. To one end is an open-plan kitchen, in the corner by the stairs a bathroom. Both sides of the partition wall are covered in framed photographs—of what appear to be his late wife and children. Some of the photographs are poster size, some bigger. He describes his occupation as 'speculative investor'.

The search was completed by mid-afternoon, the last police vehicles leaving the property at 3:48pm.

*Confidential (separate sheet)*
Funds for the extensive search were guaranteed by SCOOC. On the indoors team, as well as our own forensic team—investigating the whole building and taking fingerprints, samples, etc—were four Special Branch officers. Their sole mission was to photograph all documents found. The office was downstairs with the bedrooms.

# 25

Sister Clare,
   I will not accept. I will not accept your death. Nor will I accept my being killed.
   All this day I have been trampled over.
   Early this morning the police woke me. While I got myself up, was being polite in the kitchen—they refused coffee like it was a bribe—a helicopter went blattering back and forth over the garden.
   Of course they asked my permission first. Which I, of course, gave. (If they had an expensive piece of equipment like a helicopter standing by, then they also had a court injunction standing by to allow them to use it.)
   The place feels contaminated.
   A suited bastard, usual Mr Smooth, was in charge. He said that they'd try not to cause any unnecessary damage. And did I mind if they took away some soil samples from the recent bonfire?
   "Why?" I asked him. "What're you looking for?"
   "Bodies. Or remains of," he said. "Some local boys have gone missing."
   "What makes you think they might be here?"
   "They were last seen climbing over your wall into your woods. No-one has seen them since."
   "Look," I told him. "Look where you like."
   Fancy some country copper trying to catch me out. Twat. The helicopter has rattled and clattered the whole

day, the sound echoing back off the walls. I could feel it ripping through the leaves of the trees. The lake got ripples every which way. The moorhen and coots were terrified down there.

And that was before they got the frogmen with their orange snorkels into the water itself. (I told them that I drag the lake every winter to clear the weeds. What did they think I'd have been stupid enough to hide in there?)

Around and around went the line of policemen with their prodding sticks, and along came more policemen in clean wellies and with clean spades. And they took away soil and wet ash in plastic bags.

The helicopter, the suit said, was scanning for recently buried bodies. He told me that they can detect anything buried in the last eighteen months: the heat given off by decomposition.

And what did all this expensive equipment, what did all these expensive man-hours find? Nothing, sister. Because there is nothing here to be found.

What, though, made them think that there'd be something here to be found? Even these country coppers can't think I'm that run-of-the-mill stupid.

The only conclusion I can come to, sister, is that they have read these letters to you. (Are you, sister, to be my undoing?) Did they—whoever they are—make a copy on one of their break-ins? Easy enough these days with a scanner, then use a computer to break my very simple code. (I made the mistake back there of thinking myself too damn clever. Not again.) And, having broken my code, did they then take literally what I had meant figuratively? They are, after all, policemen.

If they have read these letters, the smooth bastard in charge made no mention of any of the gangster killings.

(Only time I've written them down is in these letters to you.) But then I've never been under direct suspicion for any of those killings. If he'd asked, he therefore would have given away the fact that he'd read these letters.

Be hard, anyway, to use a stolen copy of the letters as *prima facie* evidence. Or maybe, because I've been making up bits of the code as I go along, they haven't managed to decode all of their copy yet. (It was so new to me telling you all this that I wanted, throwing caution to the winds, to get it down quick. At times I even made a shorthand code of the code.)

They may still be investigating, looking back through their records. Won't help them much, though. Most of those cases will have been closed, the ostensibly guilty people convicted and in jail. The way the police work, they'll have done deals for most of those killings, have got 'confessions'—the 'confessors' having their co-operation taken into consideration come sentencing time. This is how the police cook their books, fix their crime-solving figures.

Smugness is not allowed here. All they'll need is the one case.

You've been the agent of my betrayal sister.

No. No, you're not. My anger is huge still. I'm angry at their stupidity—this thinking that I'm as stupid as they are. In my letter to you I mention a gun and a spade. A couple of local vandals have gone missing—therefore, they're buried here.

My anger daren't go out into the garden for a day or so. My anger, I know, will increase at sight of every broken stem, every careless footprint—I could explode out there, splatter bits of myself all over the place.

I will wait until after a storm. I'll wait a downpour to wash away the smell of them.

When the adrenalin's up, sister, one enters a
heightened state of awareness. In such a state, survival is
dependent on accurate perception. I know that you are not-
real/real; I use your eyes to see behind me.

Behind me, he made no serious attempt to read these
letters to you. (So did he already know their content? Or did
he not think this scribbled notepad worth more than a
glance?)

The outstanding question is: who were the characters
who so incompetently broke in here? They weren't police.
Were they a couple of off-duty cops, out to secure
convictions, put feathers in their caps? No. That only
happens on telly.

A couple of speculative bounty hunters? No, where's
the reward?

Not one policeman, in my hearing, mentioned these
letters. Nor would they—their copies being illicitly come
by. (The originals are now all securely tucked away in the
floor safe.)

The thing is, sister, I've trapped myself: this writing
has become important to me. I can't stop now. So what I
have to do is to make sure that these letters cannot be
chanced upon again. Consequently, I am writing this
downstairs in my office—which I've made in one of the back
bedrooms. The door to here has a droplock, which means
that while I'm in the house I can leave the writing out
without fear of forgetting that it's been left out.

A pity though—this having to write in here. Especially
this time of day. All that can be seen from here—through
the skylight—are a few leaves of one of the nearest oaks, and
some sky—at the moment, a ripple of orange-edged clouds.
Whereas upstairs, of late, I have enjoyed watching some
gulls—about seven or eight—who come to circle above the

lake. In no particular order that I have been able to make out, one of the gulls will come down between the trees—big white birds—and with the tip of one crooked wing, it will draw almost an arc upon the lake's flat surface. Then another gull will come flopping down, and trace its wing along the water in the same way.

One giveaway that they've seen these letters—they asked to see my guns. I have no licence.

"What guns?" I asked.

"Gun," he said.

"What gun?" I asked. "What would I need a gun for? What makes you think I've got a gun?"

No answer. House searched. No gun. "Why'd you burn green wood?" he asked me. I told him that it wasn't only green wood that I'd burnt, that I'd made a bonfire of old stuff, got rid of old and new together. (The broken shelter and seats: I hadn't wanted to be reminded of their vandalism, of the garden's violation.)

They didn't believe me, and went into the garden with shovels. They also picked bits of fabric out of the carpet, and took that away in little polythene envelopes. Bastards.

I will not accept sister. I will not. I need my anger as fuel to keep me going.

I am an Acceptor, sister. But I will not accept this.

Incomprehensible to me are those who, accepting their lot in life, look on the antics of the rebellious with incomprehension. I have met them and face-to-face I have tried to talk to them. We end up staring at one another with suspicious bewilderment. Why make trouble for yourself, I can see them think. Why take all life's shit, I think. I will not accept.

I will not accept your death. I will not accept your not having been. Although—and I can write this with safety now—I have had Fay and Darren and Baby Bonny's death avenged, I will not accept that all things are now equal. Wrong has been done to me again. Too many wrongs, all together.

A couple of vandals who came in here solely to smash things up got themselves lost. For that I then get coachloads of coppers trampling around my garden. Fools! Fools, all of them.

My anger knows no bounds. Nor has my anger changed. All our gut judgements are made in childhood: I am still angry from then.

Our father is out there in the wider world even now, posturing grotesquely, thinking it important to be seen with leggy young women his granddaughter's age.

And our mother? Our mother has made herself known for her 'sophisticated' legs, and is to be seen daily on the television, advertising—in soft focus—nylon tights.

If either of them get invited onto chat shows now neither of us are mentioned. Nor their grandchildren. Only the state of the film industry.

Do you know, sister—and I assume that our parents didn't know this—that twins are more likely to develop mental disorders than single-borns?

But who now, who now, would dare to question my mental health? I am too much a part of their everything. Mad they might think me, but I am too powerful to be helped. Can you imagine a Social Worker coming in here with his pink forms? No ... no, they will use letters to my dead sister to try to trap me, incriminate me. Fools! Making victims of themselves.

# 26

Steve goes to a banging at the door.

Martin is standing there, face hard in the light coming out from the hall.

"Come on." Martin turns towards the van.

"Where?" Steve doesn't move.

"Up there." Martin's anger is a taut bow inside him.

"This time of night?"

"When else do we go?"

"What we goin' for?" Steve still has his hand on the door edge.

"He's not getting away with this." Martin's index finger is levelled at Steve.

"Getting away with what? Police say there's no sign of nobody up there."

"You believe them?"

Martin has leant closer, daring Steve to contradict him.

"Look," Steve hears his voice rising, "they had infra-red scanners, all bloody sorts up there. If they can't find 'em, how can me and you?"

"Don't you care?"

"Course I care." Steve quickly responds, aware of Mary listening in the house. (Steve wishes Julie were here: she might mouth off at Martin, get him out of this.)

"One more look won't hurt then," Martin says, as if it's been decided. "Catch him off-guard."

Steve sighs, beaten down. Shaking his head—his one display of rebellion—he picks the van keys off the hook by the door.

In the van, driving what is now—even in the dark—a familiar route, ladder and board sliding around in the back, Steve says, "I still don't see the point."

"We gotta give it a chance. What else is there?"

"Missing persons list," Steve says. "Salvation Army and Red Cross put out a list."

"For fuck's sake ..." Martin clenches his anger, wants to hit Steve, right now, to swing his fist out and smash him back-handed in the face as he drives. But he knows that he can't—that he needs Steve.

"Told your missus the fuckin' police'd find nothing. Going through the fucking motions that's all. We two are the only fuckin' chance they got, poor sods."

Steve decides that Martin is mad.

Martin, for his part, doesn't know why he is so angry. He feels cheated, duped, yet knows that there is no real evidence even to suppose that the two boys disappeared in there. Apart, that is, from Nathan having once seen them going over the wall and their now being missing. Steve and the police are right, Martin knows that, realistically, the boys could be anywhere. And yet ...

Steve again stops the van by the wall. Martin pulls out the ladder, slides the board up onto the roof, climbs up into the same sycamore he has used before. Steve retrieves the board and the ladder, shoves them into the back of the van, gets his aerosol, and makes another line in the road. As before, he drives down and parks in the gateway.

Once down the other side of the wall, Martin begins his run along the woodland paths. In the dark, unseen branches whip at his body and across his face. Roots trip him, adding to his stumbling anger.

When he sees the yellow lights of the house blazing out into the night, reflected like a globe up off the lake, Martin knows the desperate futility of his being there. He will find nothing.

Brought to a stop in a clearing facing the house, he shouts his anger across at the imagined man who is making him powerless. "You murderin' evil bastard! We'll fuckin' get you yet! Think you're so fuckin' clever! You got it comin', you rich cunt ..."

Steve, walking back up the road, just as he comes level with the wall, hears Martin shouting, "... you fuckin' bastard! Don't think you fuckin' won! We'll get you for this! You murderin' evil, evil bastard!"

Standing in the middle of the road, Steve says, "For fuck's sake." He hurries back to the van.

Pausing for breath, Martin hears the beeping of the van's horn. Aware now of his vulnerability, and frightened, he begins running back through the woods. His fear makes him stumble more.

Martin sees where the van is by the reflection of its white headlights off the road and into the green leaves. Martin wants Steve to stop beeping the horn. Steve doesn't. Martin's wet soles slip off branches, and twigs catch in his hair.

"Shut the fuck up! Shut up! Shut up!" he is shouting as he climbs the tree, panting hard.

Steve has been standing by the cab, leaning in to press the horn. The engine is running, and exhaust fumes are rising through the red rear lights.

"What the fuck," Steve asks the rustling above him, "was all that shouting about?"

Martin is about to reply angrily when he falls out of

the tree onto the roof. He gasps and curses.

"Best get out of here," he says, as he scrabbles around onto the ladder. "Before he sets his fuckin' guards on us."

"What guards?" demands Steve incredulously, as he takes the board from him.

"Whatever." Martin comes down the ladder.

"Never again." Steve says as they slide the ladder in, and pull down the back. "Never a-fuckin'-gain."

"So tell me what the fuck else we do?" Martin's big face is next to Steve's as they get into the cab.

"We wait." Steve drives. "We wait for the police to find them. Like Mary wanted in the first fuckin' place."

# 27

Sister, the intruders are back.

   I can hear them out there now—in the woods on the far side of the lake, shouting obscenities at me.

   This has got to stop.

# 28

3) REPORTS (FACTUAL)

EXTERIOR

*Geophysical survey*
Large earth disturbance, cavern, by eastern wall, that of a
badger's set—tunnelling under. Rabbit warren on NE slope
responsible for other recent earth disturbance. Three graves
found 110 metres NNW of house. Bones identified as one
dog, two cats. Infra-red scan. Negative (insubstantial
differentations).

*Sub-aqua team*
Bed of artificial lake shallow, easily quartered. Nothing
found. (Subject said he clears lake of excess weed early part
of every winter.)

*Forensic analysis*
Residue in fire ash that of wood, some plastic, and
carbonised soil granules. No animal fats, bones.

INTERIOR

*Fingerprints*
Subject's own.
  One other adult male—unidentified.

*Sub-terran imaging*
One floor safe in the downstairs room used as an office.
Access granted. Stocks, share certificates, bonds only.

*Forensic analysis*
In carpet—soil and leaf debris from local woodland only.
Freezer contents—animal flesh and animal blood only.
Drains—human excrement, animal flesh and animal blood
only. Oven & hob residues—animal flesh and animal blood
only.

*Confidential (separate sheet)*
Paperwork. All photographs passed on to SCOOC and
Fraud Squad for closer scrutiny. Nil fiscal improprieties
discovered as yet. Nil criminal associations discovered as
yet. All other correspondence connected with his voluntary
counselling work. Health Authority and Social Services have
been advised of our concern over his background. Health
Authority and Social Services say they will "bear in mind"
our concerns, but that "without a criminal record to which
we can refer we are loathe to jeopardise his or our other
clients' welfare."

# 29

Dear Sister Clare,
     Today I am lost.
     I just got up from writing that and went storming
around the house—looking for something to cling my
thoughts onto. Found myself walking up and down before
the wall of family photos. Found myself shouting at all of
them. Then I tried to talk to Fay. But she is gone, really
gone. Unreachable. Mal and Ollie cannot understand me.
Every word I say is judged by them. There's only you, sister.
And I have no photos of you. So I will go now and pull out
all the old photos of me, and talk to them as if they are you.
     I forgot that I was talking to you and I found myself
studying the image in the photograph—the outer surface
that is, that was, me—was supposed to have been me. Was it
me? Truly me? I recognised it only as the image recurrent in
photos of my family. I know it's me because, in amongst
those people at that time, it couldn't have been anyone else.
     In the older photographs, of me younger, I can ponder
on that outer shell like it is some divine enigma. It is me/It
is not me. In here, with the past and the untold thoughts, is
where I am. With you/Not with you.
     What a fool I was—in that other time before this
present. What a fool am I now?
     I hate the past. All of it. Not just mine. All of
humanity's past. (A past that is but a dream partly
remembered.) My sins, sister, are insignificant compared

with the combined efforts of my fellow citizens. Those who unquestioningly belong.

Responsible people, sister—that is, those with responsibilities—never hold themselves responsible in the human or social sense. Responsible people, responsible for their families, doing responsible jobs, responsible for paying their bills, responsible for their own well-being ... they are responsible indeed. Pollution, injustice, inhumanities—all these things they help to perpetuate in their responsible positions. "Way of the world," they will say, because their responsibilities, their being responsible, is only their way of avoiding blame, of making sure that the buck passes them by. Nothing is so false as a national history. Nothing is so false as history, period.

As peoples of this world, we should all be ashamed of our pasts. None of us are innocent, or ever were innocent. That criminal past was allowed to happen. It created us. I will not accept.

I will not accept.

# 30

Steve opens the door.

"Come on." Martin gives a sideways jerk of the head.

The evening is late, streetlights glowing on red.

Steve hasn't moved: he has the set face of someone about to stand his ground. But nor does Martin say anything more. He just continues to glare expectantly at him.

"Come on where?" Steve is forced to ask.

"Up there."

"No." Steve goes to close the door. But Martin's hand is against it,

"They're up there."

"No, they're not." Steve keeps his voice low, doesn't want Mary to know.

"They are." Martin's face has come closer.

"No, they're not. We don't know where they are. Look, our kids are gone." Steve starts to nod, agreeing with the reasonableness of what he is about to say. "They could be anywhere, any city dosshouse, a doorway somewhere ... we just don't know. They could be fucking dead for all we know. What we do know is that they're not up there."

"I know they're there."

"How?"

"I know ... I know it. And I can't get over that fucking wall without your fucking van. So get me up there."

Steve is about to step back from the door, walk away and leave him standing there. But Martin reaches in and grabs Steve's shirt front, pinching the skin of his chest. "We're fuckin' goin' up there," he growls.

Steve looks into Martin's face, the round eyes so close to his own, the pear-drop smell of new sweat, the bristles on his jowls, and feels the deep ache of the pain in his chest. He can hear Mary moving in the living room. She was fast asleep in from of the telly before Martin's knock.

Julie is out. She was out last night. Mary sat at the kitchen table and cried and cried. When Julie got home she shouted at Mary because of the squashed tissues all over the floor. Then she cried, too. Steve hadn't known what to do.

Steve twists his face away to shout to Mary, "Just going out, love." Martin lets go his shirt. Steve picks his keys off the hook. "Martin wants me to pick up some timber. Won't be more than half'n hour."

"You're not ..?" she says, hesitatingly.

"Don't be daft." He doesn't look in on her.

Steve doesn't unlock the passenger door until he has reversed the van out into the road.

"We got to pick up the ladder," Martin tells Steve, getting in. Steve drives.

"I know they're up there." Martin says. Steve stops outside Martin's house.

Steve stays in the cab while Martin fetches the ladder. Martin comes to the front of the van, "The back's locked." Steve turns off the engine, tosses the keys across to him.

The back squeaks and rattles up and the ladder is slid in. Martin goes to fetch the board.

Steve can see the neighbours watching them. These neighbours will now know that Dan and Simon are missing. That makes him and Martin public property, people to be talked about and pitied. The neighbours will be puzzling over this.

The back squeaks and rattles down. Martin comes bouncing into the cab.

"Thanks for the help," he says, chucking the keys towards Steve. Bouncing off the steering wheel they hit Steve's stomach, and hurt. Steve looks hard at Martin, "This is the last time."

"Yeah, yeah." Martin gestures to the road. "Drive."

Steve is full of anger. Like a big air-bag inside him, not letting him breathe, not letting him think—beyond memory of Martin's big hand grabbing his shirt and pinching into his flesh, beyond the thud of keys hitting the side of his belly. His eyes feel fixed, like a chicken's, on either side of his nose: he can only look forward.

His driving is efficient, ruthlessly proper. He does not speak. Not even when, going through Estley, he senses Martin looking across at him and grunting contemptuously as he turns away. Steve just thinks 'cunt' and drives on up the hill.

He goes straight to the wall, pulls into the side of the road, switches off the headlights and puts on the hazard lights.

"Don't be a prat," Martin tells him.

Steve turns to stare angrily at him. He is not now afraid of the big man; or rather he is afraid, but his anger, his affront, won't let him be afraid. If only he could have been like this with Dan. And with Julie. If only he could have had this certainty.

For all that, Martin is right—in putting on the hazard lights, the orange flicking on and off, front and back, up the wall, he is being a prat. He turns them off.

"Right," Martin says. He gets out and goes round the back. And Steve knows that his uncertainty has let him be beaten again.

The shutter squeals up, ladder is slid out, then the board. As he feels Martin start up the ladder Steve gets out of the cab. The board is slapped onto the roof.

Trying to maintain his anger, Steve walks across the road and looks up at the roof. Martin is kneeling, reaching up. Once he has caught hold of a twig he stands and reaches further up into the bending branch.

Martin stops and looks around for Steve. He sees him standing across the other side of the road.

"Well, get the fucking board," he tells him.

"It can stay there," Steve says. "You got half'n hour, then I'm off."

"You stayin' right here?"

"Yeah."

"What if someone comes?"

"I'll be gone."

"You fuckin'..."

"Half'n hour." Steve looks at his watch.

Martin feels heavy. Climbing into and down out of the tree is harder this evening.

"That twat," he keeps saying to himself. "That twat."

Limping from a knock on the shin, he starts along the wall path. The sky above the woods has long rolls of clouds like pink and violet maggots.

Martin pauses where the two boys climbed over, where the heap of white fire ash was. It has been flattened now, drenched into a black oval. In the burnt out space below the trees, dusk's small, black flies rotate and zig-zag.

Martin goes on down through the woods.

All the house lights, upstairs and down, are on. Their reflection speckles off the lake.

"What now?" Martin asks himself. "What now?" What does he do now? He doesn't know. Doesn't know what he's doing here, doesn't know what he should be doing now, doing next ...

Head dropped, staring down at the barely visible black-brown ground mulch, he finds himself listening. He doesn't know what he's listening for. But, trying to shut out thought of all else, he listens.

The evening is still. The only thing moving is electricity.

What to do?

All Martin knows, here in this wood, is that all this is beyond the limits of his control. Steve is going to be gone in half an hour. And what can he, Martin Thurlow, do or say to the man inside all those yellow lights?

"My son is gone."

Is he here? Martin doesn't know. He thought he was here, he believed he was here.

"Fuck it!" he swings his big fist at a bush. The flat leaves swing aside. "Fuck it!" he kicks up into it, tearing off some leaves. "Fuck it! Fuck it!" he continues punching, kicking, stamping into twigs, stems and foliage. "Bastard. Bastard."

Out of breath, Martin stops.

Gasping, he stands a moment, almost puzzled, on top of the flattened bush. Then he turns and begins to walk up towards the wall and back to the van.

# 31

Well, sister, the switching around of routines worked. I left the house at midnight, turned left instead of right, and there on the road—in the car headlights—was a whole mess of leaves and twigs.

I drove on of course, in case they were nearby. I didn't want to let them know that I'd seen. In the very moment of seeing those green leaves and dark twigs, I figured out exactly how they'd been getting in.

They've got one of those hydraulic lifts—like they use to get up and change the bulbs on streetlights. But they didn't go over the wall with it, because then the metal of the little platform would have attracted a charge. No, from the platform, they reach instead up into a tree and then climb over the wall. They could have been using a different tree every time, and drop to the ground on my side of the wall. That's why there was no regular pathway worn, nothing for me to find.

Strange, sister, how comforting it is just knowing how they've been getting in. I was almost starting to suspect that I could have been wrong—that there was really no-one. It was the not-knowing that was spooking me. I was almost starting to believe in magic, which is the logic of desperation, where we all go when we can't find an answer.

I meet a lot of it down at 'the office'. So I know what, mentally, I was doing. Not that my confabulations had the same root cause as my clients. For them something so terrible has happened, something so out of their ordinary, that they come up with all sorts of mental bridges to reconcile the two—old with new.

I think of such mental bridges, because they're not so much conscious fantasies as prosthetic truths. Clients will start off by swearing them to be true; but such prosthetic truths are not grounded in experience. They are not therefore rooted in the person, and so the person can be argued out of them. People cannot be argued out of their experience.

What makes experience is another matter. Often, as you know, sister, faced with a problem—like these intruders—I sit and think. Just sit and frown at it. The logical deduction that comes from that sitting and frowning can move me to act. The ensuing action, however, not the reasoning that preceded it, is what will become me. Because it is the knowledge of experience that makes me act.

For instance, when young, the only son of liberal, arty types, I knew that police brutality existed and that it was wrong. And I, very properly, pitied its victims. But it was not until I was myself beaten up by the police in that cell—that time I was caught shoplifting—that I knew the shame of powerlessness and knew that what those three men did to me was absolutely wrong. No matter what I have done since, no matter what pain I may myself have caused, that experience in that police cell gave me an ideological stance, namely—a distrust of all authority—out of which I cannot be argued or persuaded.

Often, though, I don't know what my opinion on anything is until a client says something to contradict it. Then I help them examine their prosthetic truth.

You, sister, are not a prosthetic truth. I know that you're not real, not really real; but to me, you are real. For the purpose of this writing, you are a self-examining device. But you are not in any way a delusion.

Delusions, sister, are something other. They require psychiatry—but only if, unlike me, those suffering the delusions are poor. Only the poor and weak are diagnosed mad, diagnosed as clinically disturbed. For 'mad', for 'disturbed', read 'uncontrollable'. Uncontrollable, they disturb those with power—those with the power to impose order. They disturb the order, upset the power. Nowadays those with power are the rich. So, using prosthetic truths, the powerful talk the ordered into self-righteousness and have the 'disturbed' person medicated or locked away.

I, rich and therefore powerful, am not locked away because I talk to my dead, never-born sister. No, I, rich, am offered self-counselling therapies.

But I have digressed sister. I was talking of knowing. I now know how the intruders get in, and knowing is so comforting. Easy too, now, to know what to do.

All I've got to do is to find a way of getting out of the garden unseen—that is, not by the gate. I expect I'll drop a rope from one of the cedar boughs, and take the rope with me (as I don't want them using it to get in). Then I'll hide in the road outside and wait for them to come along in their hydraulic lift. Once they are identified, I can let myself back in through the gates, and get them stopped.

And that's exactly what I did, sister. Two evenings running, I got comfortable, in the late afternoon, sat behind a bramble thicket on the other side of the road. Except what came along on the second night was not a hydraulic lift, but just a furniture van. By which time it was almost dark. (Both nights I left all the house lights on as a decoy.)

The van stopped just along the road from me. And the

two men did the equivalent of what I'd guessed. The tallest climbed up a ladder onto the roof and, from there, into a tree. They weren't quiet about it either, shouting to one another with the arrogance of the stupid. For a minute, they even kept all the van lights on, which meant—their sight confined to the lights—that I could creep round the side of the bramble thicket and get close enough to read the name of a local company on the van's side—a furniture maker.

When they had gone (the tall man wasn't very long in the garden), I went over to where the van had been. I wanted to see what the driver had been doing. (All the while the tall man had been in the garden, the other man had been fussing about in the road beside the van.)

He had kicked a few leaves knocked down from the tree into the side; and on the road was a white aerosol arrow, with '18' beside it. (Was it the 18th time they'd been in? Or the day before's date?) Whatever the number, it meant that night's tree, that night's pick-up point, had been marked, should the driver and van have to leave. (And who'd have noticed another aerosol mark on the road? I hadn't. I now saw that up and down the road, each with their number, were several more white lines.)

Knowing. I now know what to do sister. I am one of the rich. People can be bought. Simple as that. I'll get someone to make these two and their van disappear.

After all the grief the pair of them have given me, I'd like to put a little fear into them first, to let them know what they're in for. Go for the top man to start with, work down to these two cretinous hired hands, and have them running scared.

But first and foremost these days I'm a businessman: I know that frightening them for the sake of it will serve no useful purpose. So, troublesome though they may have been to me, neither of them will have any reason to stay once their boss is removed. So it will have to be a simultaneous hit. No warning, just be rid of them.

And not just the two of them. I've used local firms before for that kind of work. I must assume, therefore, that that is what is being done to me. So, on the same day that these two are removed, I'll get the employer and his factory blown up. The authorities will assume that these two disappeared in the explosion, fire, whatever.

Fini.

# 32

## 4) EVALUATION/SUBJECTIVE ASSESSMENT

Never before having been in charge of such a large force, I
was nervous. This, I know, has the effect of making me
appear brusque.

The land crew having been let through the gates by
the electrician, we arrived unobserved at the house at
5:23am. We woke the suspect. That is, his bedroom light,
below the walkway to the front door, went on when we
knocked on the door and identified ourselves as police.

He certainly appeared to have just woken—the hair in
a mess, night's water-retention in the skin. When informed
that we wanted to search his house and grounds, he let us in
without hesitation.

Throughout the morning he said very little. (I had a
radio mike on to co-ordinate the search. All exchanges were
thus recorded. I, or another officer, stayed with him all the
time we were there, and everything he said was recorded at
base.)

He complained about my going to the bathroom with
him, asked if it was really necessary. Apart from that, he
made no other protest about our presence. I even had to ask
him, later, if he wanted his solicitor to be present. He asked
why.

Once he was dressed, I asked him if he had any
knowledge of two teenagers who had recently been reported

as missing. He said that he hadn't. I asked why he had cut
down the branches where the two teenagers had been seen
to climb the wall. He said that he didn't know who it was
had climbed over his wall, only that someone had, and that
they had smashed up a shelter and a seat, as well as
vandalising some young trees. I asked why he had made a
fire out of the green wood. He said that it hadn't all been
green wood. He said he had burnt only the smaller
branches, the broken seat and the shelter. He had left the
biggest branches in a stack.

He gave the appearance, although tired, of telling the
truth. But he answered only the questions asked, and
volunteered no other information. Nor did he, in any way,
attempt to ingratiate himself with me or with any other
police officer—not by a smile, not by the offer of tea. His
face remained impassive throughout.

To catch him off-guard, other officers threw in
questions. But he went even more quiet and polite. No way
was he going to be tricked into saying anything. In the end I
had to shut the others up—the more we said the more it
showed what little we knew.

His non-avoidance of eye-contact, however, I felt to
be an affectation, something practised and therefore without
meaning. It made me uncomfortable. As did the house.

Upstairs, aside from kitchen and bathroom, is one big
but sparsely furnished room. Along its lake-woodland side
are large floor-length windows. Down the centre of the
room is a partial dividing wall. On either side of this
dividing wall are huge pictures, bigger than posters, of his
dead wife and dead children; as well as his two older
surviving children and their children. He pointed out who
was who when asked.

When I asked him about his voluntary work he said

that he was sorry but it was confidential, although he did give a general outline of what it entailed. Listening to him talk of his work, I had to tell myself that this man was not made respectable by being made a victim, by his offering tea and sympathy to other victims. He is a known murderer who thinks he's gotten away with it. Bad luck for them that his wife and two of his children hadn't.

When I asked what the language was on a scribble pad on the upstairs table—the writing looked a bit like Russian symbols—he said that it was his 'twin' language, one that they'd invented and he used as shorthand for anything to do with his voluntary work.

On our way downstairs to his office I asked which was his bedroom. He said that he didn't always sleep in the same room, that it depended—literally—on which way the wind was blowing. (Alright for some.)

When, back upstairs, I saw him looking with apparent concern at the lake, I asked if he minded the divers poking about in it. He said that he dragged it every autumn, so no.

Not one question, referred to here or on the tapes, appeared to cause him the least distress.

I left the house thinking, not that here was a man with nothing to hide, rather that here was a man very much in control. And very much unafraid of us, with no reason to be afraid. As all the evidence gathered that day, and thus far processed, has confirmed.

*Confidential (separate sheet)*
I found it extremely taxing keeping him occupied while the documents in the downstairs office were being filmed. He listened carefully to all the reports coming in over the radio, to my instructions, and none appeared to cause him the least discomfort.

Faced with his politeness I became uncomfortable. Though, like him, I'm sure I didn't show it. But I did question my role in that house, my acting like a policeman, my belonging to 'the team'. In my own defence I have to say that staff shortages have been putting us all under enormous pressure. Ordinarily we would not have got funding for such a search. So, stood there, while we rooted through his life, I found myself questioning all the artificial constructs of the force used to combat the named crimes of his world. We were there, in that 'known' gangster's house, with the full machinery of the law brought uselessly to bear, because two petty thieves had gone missing. Right? Wrong? The Law? Sense?

# 33

Thoroughness, along with discipline and professionalism, are the moral concepts they adhere to. The two of them see themselves as the perfect team, look upon what they do solely as work, take satisfaction from thought-through ploys perfectly executed. (While out on any job, their professionalism has them call themselves Sid and Tel—not their real names.)

They have watched the industrial site for five days.

The actual target building is high-sided, of ridged panels, the uppermost wall panels curving up over the roof. All these panels are painted a chocolate brown. The only windows in the building, aside from six skylights, are three along the front. One of them is labelled, in red capitals, 'RECEPTION'.

Each morning the pattern has been the same. The boss, the young Mr Sweet—a small, faded man, mid-forties—arrives first and unlocks the side door. He quickly goes in, leaving it unlocked.

From the outside, Sid and Tel don't see him again until later. For the greater part of the working day, Mr Sweet and a woman sit in Reception. Both make phone calls. She types.

The woman doesn't arrive on site until just gone nine, always coming in a hurry with carrier bags taken from her car, parked in the row of three out front. Two more cars are parked in the beaten gravel and weed patch around the back.

Between Mr Sweet's arrival before eight—in a big, dull grey Mercedes, parked out front—and the woman's arrival after nine, at about five-to-eight the big man and a bent-over man come up in a blue car, which gets parked around the back. The big man is let out of the car at the front, goes in the side door and walks through to open the back door for the bent-over man. (Throughout the five days, Sid and Tel have not seen the high double doors at the back opened.)

From the noises heard shortly after eight, Sid and Tel have deduced that the big man and the bent-over man must start up the machines. (Sid and Tel have watched the front for three days from cover of a car, and for two days took turns to walk a borrowed dog along the railway path out the back—beyond the straggling buddleias and wire fence.)

At eight o'clock exactly every day, the firm's square van reverses up to the loading bay. The fat man gets out and goes in through the side door. Only on the Monday did he go first into Reception—through a door behind the desk. Every other morning, the fat man has come directly to slide back the loading bay doors, then roll up the back of the van. Sid and Tel have watched the van wobble about on its springs as the fat man has moved about inside it.

Two more men and a teenager arrive, all separately—the teenager on a pushbike—at about 8:30am.

The building being fitted with alarms, Sid and Tel haven't attempted to break in. Their guess is that the two men arriving at 8:30 work on different machines to the big man and the bent-over man.

On the Wednesday, Sid and Tel came back several times during the day. The industrial estate was busy, and no one would have noticed another car passing through. They saw the big man and the bent-over man leave half an hour before the others. The van was still out. The big Mercedes was still there.

The targets are Mr Sweet, the big man, and the fat van driver.

Sid and Tel wait until Tuesday of the next week—to ensure that the routines are the same. This Monday the fat man doesn't go into Reception.

Tuesday morning at 7:50am, Mr Sweet unlocks the side door. (If he had been late, his car held up in traffic, the job would have been postponed.)

Sid, in a blue nylon boilersuit and with a rucksack over one shoulder, goes to the side door immediately after Mr Sweet.

The door gives straight into the open space of the workshop. Mr Sweet, at a panel along the same wall as the door, is turning off the night alarms.

"Mr Sweet?" Sid says, walking towards him.

"Yes?" Mr Sweet, finished at the panel, turns towards him, his expression trying to decide what this man is doing in his factory.

The door opens to let Tel in.

Sid reaches Mr Sweet.

"You said to be here before eight."

"I did?" Mr Sweet is looking quizzically past Sid to Tel, also in a clean new boilersuit.

Mr Sweet has automatically held out his hand in response to Sid's outstretched hand. Sid takes Mr Sweet's arm by the wrist and, twisting it, he kicks his leg across the back of Mr Sweet's knees and stands on the back of his calf. Mr Sweet's torso straightens in pain.

Tel has hurried over. He drops a cheese-wire garrotte over Mr Sweet's round head. Tel stands on Mr Sweet's other calf and counts to thirty. Mr Sweet goes limp after fifteen.

(Sid and Tel have long decided not to trust this display of unconsciousness. They have also found, in practice sessions, that they can get a better purchase on the garrotte if the person is below them—with the added advantage that the person's reactions will be confused by the pain in their legs from Sid and/or Tel standing on them.)

Everything that Sid and Tel wear while on a job is dumped afterwards. Including the cheese wires and the shoes—trainers in this case. The cheese wire is cut into short sections so as to be unrecognisable as a garrotte. The trainers are disposed of in case the soles leave a traceable impact on the calves, the blood having stopped flowing around the body by the time they stand off. The guns that both have will only be got rid of if used.

Solely because of his size, the big man, they know, will present the most problems. Sid, being the bigger, is therefore to tackle him. He takes a pistol out of the rucksack should the garrotte not work.

The pistol in his right hand pocket, Sid pulls Mr Sweet's body out of sight into a panelled-off area, where the fabric fitters work. Sofas and armchairs, in dark colours, polythene-wrapped, are stacked high here, coming off a scaffold going up to the ceiling—a chain pulley for raising them hung from an iron beam painted red.

Tel has been studying the alarm panel. Mr Sweet's key bunch is still hanging from the panel door. On Sid's return, Tel points to a Fire Alarm section of the panel, and makes a turning motion.

"Try it," Sid says. Tel flicks up a chrome switch, and presses a reset button. The panel screen flashes up the message, 'Fire-fighting systems disabled'. It also begins to make a slow beeping noise.

"Need to turn off the water main too," Sid says.

Tel studies the framed building plan below the alarm panel, and looks up at the pipe sprinklers in the roof area. Still looking up, he goes towards some toilets at the back of the loading bay.

Sid takes up position behind the side door.

The alarm panel beeps. A car door slams. Sid holds both handles of the garrotte in his left hand. He is aware of a loud squeaking, metal on metal, coming from the lavatories.

The side door opens. The big man steps in. The door starts to close. The beep of the alarm has caught the big man's attention.

Sid stamps the flat of his foot into the backs of the big man's knees. Reaching out his hands for balance, the big man goes forward and down on his knees. Sid loops the garrotte over his head and pulls him back, while standing his weight on the big man's calves.

The big man has grabbed first at the wire around his throat, and realising he can get no purchase on that, he swings back his arms, trying to knock Sid off-balance. Sid arcs his own back, pulling the big man's shoulders into his knees. The big man goes limp as there is a double-bang on the back door.

Tel is by the back door, watches Sid counting, and waits.

Outside the bent-over man bangs on the door again, and shouts as well this time.

Sid pulls the big man's body towards the fabric workshop.

Tel opens the back door and, standing aside, smiles at the man.

"What took you?" the bent-over man says, stepping over the raised door sill, not realising until the door is closing that it wasn't the big man who opened it.

As he begins to turn curiously towards him, Tel trips and throws the man to the floor, where he sprawls partly face-down, partly on his side. Tel drops with both his knees onto the man's ribs and spine. He goes to slip the wire noose over the man's head. But the head is twisted awkwardly and flat to the floor; and he is trying to hit back at Tel with his left arm and kick at him with his heels.

Tel crouches close and low, grabs up the man's hair in one hand, slides the wire under his head, lets the hair go, grabs both handles of the garrotte and jerks the wire tight on the man's shout.

The van is reversing up to the loading bay.

The bent man continues to kick and thrash. Tel, hanging both-handed onto the garrotte, with his bodyweight spread to keep on top of the man and press him to the floor, still can't stop the man jerking about, and he simply looks to Sid waiting at the side door. The bent-over man, face purple, flops into unconsciousness as the side door opens.

The fat man is singing to himself, so doesn't hear the slow beep of the alarm panel. He is turning to come around the door as Sid steps past him, dropping the wire over his head, then turning to stamp into the back of his legs, and moving to stand on the back of his ankles. The fat man lands on his knees, frowning at the sight of Tel winding the wire noose out of the neck of the bent man.

While the fat man dies, Tel drags the bent man over to one of the two carpentry benches. He empties a bin of shavings and chippings beside the body, chucks some timbers down about it.

The fat man has stopped his struggles when Tel goes past him and Sid to collect the big man's body. Tel drags it by its feet. Sid follows with the fat man's body. (Had either the big man or the fat man taken a day off sick, Sid and Tel, having followed both home on Wednesday, would have gone the next day to their house.)

Sid and Tel now put the bodies together around the bench. Tel goes back for Mr Sweet's body.

Sid has emptied more shavings over the bench, and has dropped more timbers over the bodies. Tel pulls down sheets of hardboard, and slews a stack of chipboard into a fan near the bodies.

"Water off?" Sid asks.

"If that's the only rising main."

Tel flicks a lighter under some shavings. Sid lays his pistol on the bench top, unzips his boilersuit at the front, then removes it from around his wrists and ankles. He has running kit on underneath. Rolling the boilersuit up he puts it in the rucksack, and bends to take over Tel's puffing at the pile of yellow shavings.

The shavings crackle into unambiguous flame while Tel is getting out of his boilersuit. Sid gathers offcuts to add to the pile.

Tel packs the pistol, the rolled boilersuit and the garrottes into the rucksack, tightens the drawstring, and does up the buckles. Watching the flames, Sid helps Tel into the straps.

They nod to each other and go to the back door. Smoke is beginning to coil in around the roof space. The skylights are closed. Orange flames are now about a metre high, should soon spread through the scattered timber and boards to the racks and stacks against the walls.

Sid and Tel close the back door behind them.

It is nine minutes past eight. It is another twenty minutes before anyone else arrives, leaving sufficient time for the fire to take hold. In their earlier contingency planning, Sid and Tel talked of dropping the latch on the side door to give themselves more escape time before the 8:30am discovery of the bodies.

This was decided against, as soon as both realised that they would have the camouflage of a fire. The side door being locked might then have aroused suspicion. Now, when the door is casually opened, the inrush of air will boost the blaze; the same with the back door.

The padlock on the gate to the railway bank had been cut by Sid last week. Now they remove the padlock and take it with them, as they pick their way up the embankment.

Once on the path above the railway—curving away from the industrial estate—they begin jogging. Neither look back. Both are already flushed from their exertions.

The railway runs around by the motorway link road. Their car is parked among others in a long lay-by there. Sid and Tel know that no-one saw them leave the factory. There is nothing else to connect them with it.

For a multiple killing of this kind, the death of one bystander, in their reckoning, is pretty good going. With the added bonus too of it, at least initially, looking like an accident. Because, even if the authorities are suspicious, by the time they form their suspicions, Sid and Tel will have been given that much more of a headstart—security videos will have been taped over, memories will be smudged—than would have been the case from an obvious and dramatic hit.

Within twelve minutes of leaving the building they are on the motorway heading North.

The agent will transfer the second half of their fee as soon as she receives independent confirmation of the execution.

# 34

Why, sister, is life held to be so important? Aside, that is, from the obvious, if-we-weren't-here-to-see-it-we-wouldn't-know-about-it. But why else is it so important?

What is life? I have watched singers, their eyes closed, living a whole life inside the sounds they are making. I have watched guitarists too, and double-bassists, existing in the tips of their fingers. But, the truth of it is, those are only moments. And they are exceptional people.

Most people don't live their lives as if their lives were important to them. They put up with stupid jobs, poor wages, and bad marriages, and live in houses and places they loathe. They spend most of their lives doing what they don't want to do. Only at the point of death, only made aware of the inevitability of their death, do they begin to value their life. (Some people's lives are only valued for their deaths: a life built backwards from the mode and moment of death— murder victims, usually.)

In that instant, they want life at any cost, sister, no matter what they do with their lives. Threatened with death, they will crawl, beg, plead, promise anything—provided they are allowed to stay alive. But to live what kind of life? Simply to be alive? Is that enough?

What is life, sister? For instance, up there, diagonally across what I have just this minute written, is a brown smear—another mosquito's life I have accidentally smudged out. Who mourns that? Who cares?

What is life? I have no answer, sister. I cannot make a judgement. People just are. Or are not. You have been, too, without knowing you have been alive. What is life?

Finally, I accept, and I watch other lives.

No, I don't accept. I am dissatisfied with this life, with the absences about me in this life.

This existence of mine is not enough, sister. I have sometimes, often, thought you were lucky in that you were spared life. Then I think that if you'd been here, then this life for both of us would have been different, and I wouldn't be here thinking these thoughts.

Is that what keeps us holding on to life, sister? The chance that it may become different? As small a chance as that may be, we can still dream, can still—being alive—live other lives inside our minds. (Is that why the destruction of dreams, of delusions, of people's small distant hopes, is often held to be a greater crime than actual murder? Is that why truth-tellers are so despised?)

My problem now is that I have no other lives inside my mind. Oh, I'd like to be reconciled to the children, to see my grandchildren. But it won't satisfy, will not fulfil a dream. And a dream is never enough. Reality it has to be.

There have been times in my life, sister, when I have been so sensitive to what was happening about me, it was like my skin had been peeled away and I could feel the slightest change in the air, the most subtle inflexion of mood, the thoughts of insects, the edge, the very delicacy of life. Exhilarating, at moments, it may have been. But it was not a happy state, sister. It hurt. It fucking hurt.

Now it is different. Now I am withdrawing from that outer surface. Now that wrinkled, deadened shell serves only as insulation. No longer am I raw to the world. But neither is this insulated isolation a happy state. Rawness is preferable to this inertia, to this nothing-matters numbness.

Life, sister, the life others were living, and that I was living, was forever at a remove. Even pain was a third party event, viewed from inside and outside but never from within the pain itself. At times—even with Fay and the children—I used to act out emotions, in the hope that from the act I might come to feel something genuine.

I know that I am not the only one like this. In the artificiality of most lives, in the self-creation of a history and an identity, is the feeling that life has happened to them when they weren't ready for it.

They hang on to the few solid kernels of real-ness. The biological process of ageing is real. The rest feels, they say, as if it has been organised about them, is not of their making, that the decisions they thought they had made are, in retrospect, the only decisions that could have been made. They felt that events happened to them, were merely channelled through them, and so were made their life. Yet it was their life, the only life they are ever going to know.

Dissatisfied with my whole life, dissatisfied the whole of my life, I have occasionally thought that I may have been better off having been born poor, with having had something definite to struggle towards. But as I wished it, sister, I saw such wishing as the nadir of stupidity.

It's easy to be rich, sister, to feel at home with wealth. Anyone who tells you otherwise has got other problems. Having enough money is never a problem.

Money, for instance, takes care of my sexual pleasures. People offer themselves for sale for all sorts of purposes. People can be bought, simple as that. I have money.

Nor am I owned by my possessions. I know that—ultimately—all that I can own is my own mind, and that only just.

To be a part of something, to belong to something, is all that I have ever wanted, since you were born dead. And I belong to here now, have a life now—my voluntary work, and my garden.

Still, I feel that I am living on the edge of my own existence, an adjunct to my own life among others. This momentary speck of existence, massive as my years, but minute among millions—at every twist and turn of my life, I have tried to give it meaning. Intellectual masturbation. I am a masturbating metaphysicist.

All of which is why I now try to avoid feeling.

When I have finished writing to you, all that I will be left with is routines. Barren of thought, day to day, I will move between routines. And, out of the mud of those future days, will come an event. I'm almost going to miss the intruders. All that I return home to now is sadness.

I do want, sister, but it is a formless want. I want something more than talking to myself on paper. What though? Nothing that I can point to and say that this is what I want. Yet still I go on living.

I'm this old and still I'm looking for something, sister. And I still don't know what it is. Is it still you?

# 35

*(from page 5 of 'The Mercury & Express')*

## Double Tragedy For Two Hambrook Families

For the families of two of Sweets fire victims, Steve Flinthorn and Martin Thurlow, tragedy struck again this week with the discovery of the bodies of their sons, Daniel Flinthorn (15) and Simon Thurlow (15). Both bodies were found in an overturned car on MOD land. It is assumed that they were using an old runway to do skid turns, when the car overturned and ended upside-down in a waterfilled ditch.

*Car stolen*

The overturned car, a Renault 22, belongs to Ms Hannah James of Hambrook, and was reported stolen over a month ago. The bodies of the two boys are thought to have been there at least three weeks. An MOD spokesperson said that there was an internal investigation under way to discover how the two boys could have gained access to a "highly sensitive site" and how the overturned car could have remained undetected for over a month.

*Sweets blaze*

Given the ferocity of the blaze, anxieties continue to be expressed over the effectiveness of fire-retardation materials used by Sweets Suites. A spokesman for Sweets Suites claimed that all materials accorded with current safety requirements. The spokesman declined to comment further on the blaze—which caused damage to adjoining properties—and said that they were awaiting the Fire Officer's report. The bereaved families were offered counselling.

Printed in the United States
15779LVS00001B/23